# TH_
# RELUCTANT
# SPY

# THE RELUCTANT SPY

## MIKE LOWE

FEEDAREAD
*www.feedaread.com*

Published in 2024 by FeedARead.com

Copyright © Mike Lowe

A CIP catalogue record for this title is available from the British Library.

# 1

A tall slim man in his early thirties, with sandy coloured hair and pale blue eyes, dressed in the city gent's uniform of black jacket and striped trousers, but without the customary bowler hat, walked slowly alongside the lake in one of London's beautiful inner-city parks, admiring a scene that was very familiar to him as he often walked there in his lunch hour. His name was Steven Sebworth, but it was known to very few people.

It was cold, still the tail-end of winter; a chilly wind made Steven pull his jacket more tightly around him.

He was enjoying this brief respite from his office where he worked as a procurement officer in the Ministry of Defence in Whitehall. He felt trapped in a boring job with little or no prospects. He longed to get away and do something interesting, but he was desperately shy, would never speak up for himself, would never dare to ask for an upgrade.

Ordering office supplies and the ephemera of government was tedious. The job paid well but he considered himself a failure. His father had wanted him to work in the city as he had himself. The old man had been proud to be a city gent, although he never talked about his work. Steven suspected it was in one or other of the ministries.

Whenever he could, Steven left the office to get a breath of fresh air, usually in St. James' Park, which was only a few minutes-walk from his office.

Sometimes he would visit the Stanley Gibbons stamp shop in The Strand. He rarely bought anything – stamps were so expensive, but he liked to browse. His own modest collection gave him a great deal of pleasure.

As he rounded a bend in the path, he was delighted to see that his favourite seat next to the lake was unoccupied and he quickened his step before someone else claimed it. He sat down with a contented sigh.

The weak sunlight reflecting off the water lit the colourful plumage of the mallards as they squabbled for the few scraps of bread that remained from an earlier bagful, given by old Henry, caretaker of one of the ministry buildings, who fed the birds every day.

Steven smiled at the aggressive behaviour of the ducks, thinking that they were not really very nice, despite their popularity among humans.

A foreign looking young man, dressed in a badly cut dark suit, came and sat beside Steven. He didn't say anything, just sat staring at the water.

In a sudden fit of silliness, Steven whispered, 'Have you got the money?' He had fantasised about re-enacting a sketch he had seen on the television, but he regretted it as soon as he had spoken. But the man answered, in an eastern European accent.

'What is password?'

Steve assumed the man was playing along with the game and said, 'Serpentine', the name of a lake in another park that Steven often visited, it was the first word that came to mind.

'That was yesterday, change every day. Suppose is OK. Have you got it?' whispered the man.

'Money first,' said Steve. This is great, thought Steven; the guy must have seen the sketch.

'I need stuff,' said the man.

'Six o'clock this evening, under the clock in St. Pancras station. Now where's the money?' Steve tried not to laugh.

'OK, you better be there! In waste bin,' he said, indicating an adjacent receptacle. 'In brown envelope. Don't get till I gone.' He sat for a few more minutes, not looking at Steven and saying nothing, then got up and walked briskly away.

Steven was smiling. Fancy, a complete stranger playing along with his game.

He looked at the waste bin, fantasising again. Supposing there really was an envelope full of money? He grinned and chuckled, covering his face in case anyone saw him. Although there were no people near enough to see what he was doing, he got up and surreptitiously rummaged in the bin among the banana peels and assorted rubbish.

'My God! There is an envelope!' he exclaimed. He hadn't seen the man put the envelope in the bin; he hadn't noticed him until he had sat down.

Looking around, to be sure he had not been seen, he took the envelope and put it inside his jacket before sitting again. He sat for a few minutes watching the birds, waited until a group of youngsters had noisily passed by before taking out the envelope.

Inside was a thick wad of twenty-pound notes. He suddenly went cold, his hands trembled as he looked at the notes, trying to estimate how much money was there. There must be at least a couple of thousand pounds, he thought, but it was difficult to guess with the new plastic notes as they were so tightly packed together.

'Now what do I do?' he muttered to himself, quickly stuffing the envelope into an inside pocket. Feeling conspicuous, he stood up and headed back to his office.

He hurried along the corridor, hoping he would not see any of his colleagues, and once safely in his office he closed the door and sat at his desk, slightly out of breath.

He took the envelope and pushed it to the back of a drawer in his desk and moved several oddments in front of it, then took it out again and looked inside. He hadn't imagined it, the money was there. He put the envelope in the drawer again, shutting it firmly. He looked at his telephone. Should he tell the police? They wouldn't believe him, would they? But he could not just ignore it.

'Whatever's the matter, Mr Sebworth?' asked Lydia, his secretary, when she came in with a tray of tea and biscuits later in the afternoon. 'You look pale, are you all right?'

'I don't feel very well, Lydia, I don't know what it is.'

'Shall I call for a doctor?'

'No, no. That won't be necessary. I'll be all right I expect. Cup of tea should do the trick.'

'What about a drop of something in it?' Lydia suggested, leaning close and looking worried.

'I don't have anything to put in it.'

He always felt uncomfortable when Lydia came close, her dark, almost black hair and blue eyes fascinated him but he was never easy in the presence of women and this one particularly was very feminine indeed. As she leaned closer, he could smell her perfume.

He had never had a close relationship with a woman. His mother had died in childbirth; his father had looked after him until he was old enough to be packed off as a boarder to a minor public school.

Apart from the fearsome matron at school, his secretary was the first woman with whom he had any contact at all. Even at university his friends were all men, and they tended to be the bookish sort as was he.

He avoided getting too close to Lydia.

'Mr Fergussen, who was here before you, left a bottle of brandy, and I kept it just in case it was needed for medicinal purposes. Shall I get it?'

'Yes, please do, Lydia. It might help.'

Lydia returned with the brandy and poured a generous slug into Steven's cup.

It didn't help, in fact the spirit made him feel sick. He was sweating and felt really uncomfortable.

'Lydia!' he called, 'I think I had better go home. I might be sickening for something.'

'Very well, shall I tell Mr Cartwright?'

Cartwright was the head of Steven's department, and a stickler for correct procedure in every aspect of the job.

'Yes, better do that. Thanks, Lydia. I'll hope to come in tomorrow.'

He took the money from its temporary hiding place and put it securely in an inside pocket, patting it and hoping nobody would stop him on his way out and ask if anything was wrong. He left the office without speaking to anyone.

He hurried to the Westminster Underground station in Bridge Street, where he boarded an unusually empty train on the Circle Line. Not usually travelling at this time of day, he was surprised to find a choice of seat.

He looked at his fellow passengers, wondering what they were thinking about. All he could think about was the thick wad of money in his pocket. It felt much bigger than it was and he was sure people were looking at the bulge in his jacket. The tattooed young man sitting opposite was staring at him. He wished he had thought to wear his raincoat.

He left the Circle Line at South Kensington and boarded a similarly empty Piccadilly Line train.

When the train stopped at Kings Cross St Pancras he got off, instead of going on to Bounds Green, the station nearest to his lonely little flat in Elvendon Road in Palmers Green.

He wanted to see if anyone turned up at six o'clock. It was only just gone four when he entered the great atmospheric train-shed of St Pancras, now sadly without the sounds and smells of steam engines that he had loved in his youth. But the excitement of the big station was still there. He made for a bar and ordered a lager.

He was still feeling queasy and lager was not the best choice. After a few sips, he left it and headed instead for the Benugo Espresso bar on the Grand Terrace from where he could see the great clock, under which he had instructed his mysterious contact to wait.

'This is ridiculous', he said to himself, as he took his double espresso from the barista. He took a seat and prepared to wait.

After half an hour spent watching people come and go, wondering who they were and where they were going, Steven was bored. He got up, meaning to forget the whole thing and go home.

But, looking at the big clock again, he decided to see it through. He bought a paperback from WHSmith's and returned to the coffee shop.

The book, one of Scott Mariani's, was gripping from page one, and helped pass the time.

The next time he looked at his watch it was twenty minutes to six. He was beginning to feel anxious, supposing the man did come, then what? He should tell the police, but such a story – would they believe him. He had the money, surely proof enough.

While he was debating with himself, he saw the man from the park, pacing up and down under the clock, looking at his watch and then up at the clock, every few seconds. He was clearly anxious.

Making sure he could not be seen, Steven took a quick snap of the man with his phone.

Two men, dressed in navy blue overcoats, entered the coffee bar and headed straight for Steven.

'Would you please come with us – quietly,' said the first man, while the other one took hold of Steven's arm.

'What!' exclaimed Steven.

'Quietly please, we don't want a fuss,' said the first man, evenly.

'Who are you, what do you want?'

'You'll see. We need to get away from here.'

'I demand to know who you are?'

'You are in no position to demand anything. We are government agents. Just come quietly.'

There was nothing Steven could do. People were looking, but nobody came to his assistance.

He allowed himself to be led outside where he was none too gently pushed into the back seat of a large black car. The two men got in, one in front beside the driver and the other in the back with Steven. The car started up and drove off into the traffic. Despite his situation he was annoyed to have left his book behind.

He looked around him, Jaguar F Pace; not like a proper Jaguar, he thought to himself,

'OK, now we can talk,' began the man sat beside him. 'We are MI5,' he quickly showed a badge in a little black folder. 'We have been watching you.'

'What? Watching me, why?'

'You know very well why; we just want to know who you are working for.'

'If you've been watching me, you'll know I work for the government – Ministry of Defence.'

'Who gave you the money?'

Steven was shocked. They *had* been watching him.

'It was all a mistake, I was playing a game – something I saw on the television, but it turned out not to be a game.'

'What do you mean, a game? You gave the password. How do you explain that?'

'I just said the first thing that came into my head.'

'What was it?'

'Serpentine.'

'Who gave you the password?'

'Nobody, I told you, I made it up.'

'But it *was* the password.'

'He said it was yesterday's password, but he accepted it.'

'So how did you know the password?'

'I refer you to my previous answer,' said Steven, boldly. 'He asked if I had the stuff, and I said, money first – I was still playing the game and I thought it was great that this stranger was playing along with me.'

'And he left the money?'

'He said it's in the rubbish bin. I said meet me at six o'clock under the clock at St Pancras. It seemed suitably theatrical.'

'And he accepted that?'

'He said I had better be there. Then he left. After a few minutes I looked in the bin and sure enough there was the money.'

'If you thought it was a game, why did you look in the bin?'

'I don't know.'

'I don't believe a word of it.' said the man in the front seat.

'We'll get him back to the office and get the truth out of him,' said the man beside Steven. 'Oh, you'd better give me the money. How much is it?'

'I haven't counted it, a couple of thousand I guess,' said Steven, handing over the envelope.

'Not much to risk your neck for, is it?'

'I didn't know what I was getting into.'

'So you say.'

# 2

The car stopped outside an anonymous looking building in a side street in Soho. Steven recognised the area as he had worked for a short time after leaving school for a life assurance company in Ingestre Place, near the famous Berwick Street market.

'Out!' commanded the man beside him.

The man who had ridden in the front came round and grabbed Steven's arm again. 'This way,' he said, sharply.

Steven was hustled up a flight of uncarpeted, dusty stairs and pushed into a room where the only furniture was a single wooden chair and a small square table.

'Sit,' commanded one of the men. Steven couldn't see either of them as they were behind him, and he couldn't distinguish between them, they sounded alike, although one was very much bigger than the other.

They both appeared in front of him as he sat. Unaccountably he felt he should give them names. He decided on Robin and Rodney. He smiled.

'What's so funny?' asked Robin, scowling.

'Nothing.'

'Right, now start from the beginning,' said Rodney.

'What do you mean?'

'Are you going to make this difficult?'

'Not necessarily.'

'Look, if you get clever, we can get nasty,' said Robin. 'Answer the questions and you'll be all right.'

'I told you what happened. I had seen a sketch on the television in which a man was sitting on park bench when a man came and sat beside him and asked if he had the money. I always wanted to try it and this time I did. The other man seemed to be playing along – I thought he must have seen the TV sketch. It was fun!'

'But you knew the password!' Robin shouted, banging his hand on the table.

'It was a pure coincidence. I could have said anything. I was still thinking the guy was playing. Don't you see? If he was play-acting, he would accept any word I said, and he did.'

'If what you say is true, and I don't think it is, you understand, but if it is, where is the man the Russian was supposed to meet? Tell me that. You were the man he was scheduled to meet – weren't you!' Robin banged the table again, making Steven jump.

'I don't know, he must have seen me talking to the guy and backed off. I didn't see anyone else. And if you were watching me, you must have seen there was nobody else. It was a cold day; the park was almost deserted.

'There wasn't anyone else because you were the contact. That's right, isn't it?' insisted Robin.

Steven didn't answer. There was no point.

'Right, let's have a look at the money,' said Rodney, taking the envelope from his pocket. 'Did you count it?'

'No, I haven't counted it. I haven't touched it.

'That's good, we might be able to get some fingerprints,' said Rodney. 'Here – bag it,' he said, handing it to Robin.

'Had you dealt with this man before?'

'No, of course not.'

'Who did you deal with before? Did you know his name?'

'There was no before. I've never done anything like this before. It's all a mistake I tell you.'

'What is your job in the ministry?' demanded Robin, coming face to face with Steven.

'I'm a procurement officer, only a very small cog in the wheel.'

'But you must handle all sorts of secret information.'

'Not really, I deal mainly with office supplies and furniture.'

'What about military equipment?'

'I've sourced office equipment for Army bases and so on.'

'But you have access to military information.'

'I suppose someone in the office probably deals with that sort of thing, but I don't know who it might be.'

'But you could find out?'

'Look, what are you getting at? I know nothing about any sensitive material, this has all been a silly mistake. I'm not a spy, I'm just a sort of glorified clerk. Who are you, anyway. You've no right to treat me like this.'

'That's where you are very wrong, my friend. We are government, MI5, we can do what ever we like. We answer to nobody, understand?' He paused. Letting that information sink in. 'Now, what I am suggesting is that you have access to material that could be of interest to a foreign power.' Rodney looked Steven closely in the face, making him feel uncomfortable.

'Only if they wanted to know where we get our paperclips from,' quipped Steven.

'Don't try to be clever with us, Mr Sebworth. This is serious, and you are in serious trouble.' This was Rodney, who had not said as much as his partner so far.

'You could easily get useful information if you wanted, surely?' said Robin. The two men were taking it in turns to fire questions and Steven was getting very agitated.

'No, no, I told you, I have no access to sensitive material.'

'But you know where it is kept.'

'I've never given it a thought.'

'Come on now, we caught you red-handed. Best tell us all about it. It will be better for you in the end.' Rodney had softened his voice now, trying to sound friendly.

Steven didn't answer and the two men left the room. The sound of the door being locked seemed ominously loud.

It was very quiet and Steven was getting very anxious. He now realised he was in serious trouble. He looked around the bare room. There was only one door and the window had bars. He looked out onto the street. There were people and cars below, but there was no way he could call for help. It was beginning to get dark.

Surely, they are not going to leave me here all night, he thought.

Two hours later and still no sound from his captors. The little patch of sky visible from the window was now almost black.

They are going to leave me here, Steven said to himself. I'm hungry, and I need the loo!

Just as Steven was contemplating using a corner of the room as a urinal, a noise outside made him stop.

The two men burst into the room, looking very intimidating.

'Right!' said Rodney. 'Where were we?'

'I'm about to pee in my pants if you don't allow me to go to the loo,' said Steven, boldly.

'Oh, of course,' said Robin, 'of course, come with me.' He took Steven's arm and led him from the room and along a dingy corridor.

'There, don't try anything,' he said pushing Steven through a door marked WC.

The toilet was tiny, consisting only of a bare pedestal with no seat. There was no window and no washing facility, but having relieved himself, Steven felt a little better. He was still very worried about his situation and still hungry.

'I want something to eat and drink,' he said to Robin, who then led him back to the room where Rodney waited.

'Can we get something sent up?' Robin asked Rodney.

Rodney spoke briefly on his mobile phone.

'OK, coming up. Now, let's get on.'

'There's nothing to get on with,' said Steven. I've told you what happened. You've got the money. I'll just have a bite to eat and I'll leave you two gentlemen to your spying, or whatever it is you do.' Steven had spoken boldly, and for a moment his interrogators were silent, surprised at Steven's audacity.

'Not so fast! We haven't finished with you, my lad, not by any means,' began Rodney, 'You will answer our questions and then you will no doubt be charged with espionage and jailed, probably for a very long time, understand?'

This frightened Steven and he nodded meekly.

'Good, said Robin, 'Now. What we want to know is who your contacts are and when and where you have arranged to meet.'

'Oh, God!' Steven exclaimed, 'I've told you. I have no contacts. It was all a silly game.'

'Then why did you go to the station at the time you told the man in the park to meet? Tell me that!'

'I was still playing the game, although obviously I realised there was more to it after I found the money. I thought about going to the police, but thought they wouldn't believe me.'

'No, they wouldn't, any more than we do. Look Steven, may I call you Steven? I don't want this to be any worse than necessary, but if you don't cooperate it will get very nasty, do you understand?' Robin spoke quietly, but the menace was still there.

The door opened and a young man came in with a cardboard box and a can of Coke. 'That's three pounds fifty,' he said.

'You got any money?' asked Robin.

'You expect me to pay for it?' asked Steven.

'Yes, you asked for it.'

'Very well,' said Steven feeling in his pocket for change. 'There you are, chum, and that's for your trouble,' he said handing the lad an extra pound.

'Cheers, Guv,' said the lad.

'Now can we get on!' said Robin sounding impatient.

'When I've finished my burger if you don't mind.'

'This is ridiculous,' said Rodney to Robin as they watched Steven munching his burger. 'We're not getting anywhere.'

'Do you think he would act this way if he really was guilty?'

'I'm beginning to wonder. What do you say, up the ante a bit?'

'Could do, but careful, just in case.'

Steven had finished his burger and was drinking his cola, when the two men turned to him again.

Without warning, Robin struck Steven hard on the side of his head, almost knocking him off his chair and sending his can spinning across the bare wooden floor, spraying Coca Cola in a wide arc.

'Hey! What was that for?' gasped Steven, holding his head.

'That's just for starters. If you don't help us there will be a lot more, and a lot worse.'

'You can't do that! Torture is illegal.'

'Who are you going to tell?'

Another punch, this time to his stomach, left Steven doubled up in pain, and having difficulty breathing.

Robin appeared to be enjoying himself as he approached Steven again, punching his fist into his palm with a menacing sound. A sound that would be made when he hit – and he did, the other side of his head this time.

Steven slumped in his chair, beathing heavily, gasping through the pain.

Robin hit him again, on his shoulder, making his whole arm numb.

Rodney pulled him upright in his chair, came close and looked him in the eyes.

'Now, listen to me. My friend can go on hitting you, he likes it, he's a right bloody bastard', he smiled and turned to his colleague. 'Right Bastard!' He smiled again and Robin smiled. They had done this routine before. Probably many times.

'Now, Steven. I can make it stop. Just tell us what we want to know.'

# 3

Steven was surprised when, after a lot more questions and threats, but mercifully no more beatings, the two men had nodded to each other and told him he could go. But only if he did something for them.

They had even called a taxi for him.

Back home, Steven was so tired he went straight to bed and slept.

When he woke at seven o'clock the next morning, he thought for a moment that the whole experience had been a dream. But when he felt his head and his shoulder and saw the bruise on his abdomen, he knew it was not. He felt removed from reality somehow. This couldn't be happening to him.

Later, sitting in his office he was still in something of a daze. Hardly able to believe what had happened.

'Are you hungry, Mr Sebworth?' Lydia asked, smiling. 'You've eaten nearly all that pencil!'

Steven looked at the chewed end of his pencil and at his secretary who was looking at him with concerned affection. 'I was just thinking,' Steven muttered.

'Are you sure you're all right? You shouldn't have come in today; you weren't well yesterday. Why don't you go and see the doc?'

'Mm? Oh, no, I am all right really, thanks,' said Steven, chewing his pencil again.

'I'm worried about you. Why don't you take some time off?' Lydia hovered close to Steven.

'What? Time off? What are you talking about?

Steven tried very hard to look as if he hadn't a care in the world, but failed. Lydia came closer. She had grown very fond of Steven but had resisted giving him any indication. Close relationships between staff really weren't the done thing in this sort of establishment. But try as she might to hide her feelings, she could not. She noticed him wince when she touched his shoulder and let her hand slide down his arm to his hand. She was afraid he might tell her to leave him alone, but she persisted. Steven looked up at her and took hold of her hand, gripping it tightly.

'I'm in trouble, Lydia. Big trouble. I don't know what to do.'

'Oh, Steven!' she had never called him by his first name before, 'can I help?'

'No, I don't think so. Nobody can.'

'Can you tell me about it? You know what they say – a problem shared – you know?'

'I can't involve you; it could be very dangerous.'

'Dangerous! Please tell me. I might be able to help,' Lydia pleaded. She looked at him closely, longing to be able to help.

Steven desperately wanted to tell her, but he dare not.

***

He stared at the big clock and at the space underneath, waiting for someone to appear. The MI5 men had insisted on him making the rendezvous again. Steven argued that as he had failed to hand over the documents as arranged, the man wouldn't come again.

Despite the anxiety of his mission, Steven felt a reminiscent thrill when he once more entered the huge echoing train-shed with its incredible glazed roof. This was where he had been taken as a child when returning to school after vacations. It was all different now of course.

A large envelope containing the blue-prints he had taken from the waste bin in the print-room was tucked inside the lightweight raincoat he had bought from Austin Reed only recently. It was easier to conceal the envelope in a coat. He didn't want to be seen with an official looking package – it might look suspicious. But then, a nervous looking man with his hand inside his coat like Napoleon didn't look suspicious. He actually smiled at that thought.

He was thinking about the blue-prints. He'd chosen them because he thought they looked more authentic than plain black and white documents but he had no idea what device was depicted in the faded drawings. They had been rejected as poor-quality prints and would not be missed.

If the man was coming, he was late. Steven looked anxiously at the big clock and at his watch, which agreed it was eight minutes past six.

Then he saw him, the man from the park, looking very furtive and also looking at the big clock.

Steven emerged from his hiding-place behind a news stand.

'Oh, there you are! Have you got it?' said the man, breathlessly. 'I afraid you not come and I am go to high jump.' He smiled grimly at the image his phrase conjured.

Steven reached inside his coat, but the man stopped him. 'Not here, we get coffee. You slide under table.'

They made for the brightly lit 'Café Bar' and Steven bagged a table while his co-conspirator went to order. 'What you want?' he said.

'Get me anything.'

While he was away, Steven realised that the man was at least as nervous as himself. They were just messengers, doing the dirty work of dangerous people.

'Here, I got double espresso,' said the man as he sat down and placed two tiny cups on the table. 'You want eat?'

'No, I couldn't eat a thing,' said Steven, managing a smile.

'Hand over then,' said the man.

Steven slid the package under the table and the man took it and transferred it inside his own coat.

'Do you know what is?'

'No idea, came from the secret department,' Steven improvised.

'Good. I hope they satisfied. Blame me if stuff I get is not pukka.'

Steven suddenly felt sorry for the man. He stuck out his hand across the table, 'I'm Steve, what's your name?'

'Wassily', said the man, nervously taking Steven's hand.

'Good to meet you, Wassily, where are you from, Russia?'

'No!' he said, emphatically, 'Ukraine, but I work for Russians, to my shame.' He laughed, a short humourless bark. 'New to this game, are you?'

'Yes,' said Steven, not sure what else he could say.

'Have they got you do this against will?

'Yes. They have.'

'Who are they, can you say?'

'Not really, I'm not too sure who they are.'

'It is nasty business. Try get out if you can,' advised Wassily. Steven was warming to the man.

'I guess we'd better go,' suggested Steven.

'Yes. Take care, Comrade. I hope we don't meet again.' He smiled and did a little salute before leaving the table and merging among the commuters.

# 4

Having completed the task, Steven was once more sitting behind his desk, faced with a pile of files which needed his attention. He ignored them. He could not think about his work. His head was in a spin; the meeting in the park, the money, the MI5 men, the blue-prints, Wassily – they were all going round and round, making him feel confused.

What is going to happen now, he asked himself. What would the MI5 men do now? They said they would be watching the transaction and would follow the man Steven now knew as Wassily, hoping to find his contact. Steven worried about him; he seemed a nice man, doing a job he didn't want to do. Who were his masters? Did they pose a threat to the country? Of course they did, if they were accessing secrets. And now he was one of them. What – a spy? Literature had coloured the term and it seemed unreal.

Suppose the blue-prints were important. They had been in the waste bin; all the rejected copies would be destroyed, maybe at the end of the day. But then it suddenly occurred to him, wouldn't there, more than likely, be a record of spoiled copies? The thought made Steven feel sick.

Lydia came into the office with his morning coffee and biscuits.

'My Goodness! Mr Sebworth, Steven, whatever is the matter, you look dreadful. Why don't you go to see the medic.' She referred to the in-house doctor, whose surgery was in their building.

'I'm all right, Lydia, really, or I will be when I've had a cup of coffee. This business has taken it out of me.' Steven looked up at his secretary who was leaning close and looking very worried.

Since telling Lydia that he had a problem that he wanted to share, but couldn't, he had become more aware of her, and now when she came very close, he realised with some surprise that he was attracted to her.

'You aren't all right, Steven, I can tell. What has happened? You can't go on like this. What are you going to do?' Lydia asked.

'No, you're right, but what *can* I do?' And then it all came out; he couldn't help it. 'I have committed a very serious crime, Lydia, treason. Treason! Do they still hang you for treason? Oh God!' He clung on to Lydia, almost in tears, shaking.

Lydia did her best to calm him, speaking softly and stroking his hair. He gradually got himself together and apologised. Lydia smiled, but she was also near to tears, seeing Steven so distressed. She felt helpless.

He hadn't explained the circumstances of his crime and Lydia had not asked. He vowed to be more careful what he said in future. Lydia was not likely to forget what he'd told her, but maybe she would have put it to the back of her mind.

Despite his fears, but needing to clear his head, Steven took his usual walk in the park at lunchtime, he didn't see the trees and the flowers and the ducks. They were there, but all Steven could see was a dark-suited man, standing by his favourite seat, waiting for him. As he got closer, he could see it was the man he called Robin.

He approached cautiously.

'Ah, Steven! So good to see you. Well done old man. You did your job perfectly. We were able to follow your contact and find his boss. He's helping us now!' He laughed, not a nice sound.

Steven knew all too well what 'helping' meant. The poor man was being beaten and kept without food or water.

'Now, we've got another little job for you.'

'Oh, no, no more,' Steven pleaded.

'Yes, of course, you are very useful to us.'

'I don't want anything to do with it, I tell you. It was all a big mistake. Now, let me go.'

Robin now spoke more sternly, holding tight onto Steven's sleeve. 'Listen to me. You have no choice. You're in now, like it or not. You could go to the police, I suppose, but we would have to tell them that you have been passing sensitive information to an enemy.' He smiled grimly. 'Do you know what they do with spies? No, well I'll tell you. After the interrogation, you will be put on trial, that's just a formality, the conclusion is inevitable – you will be found guilty and put in prison – for life.'

Robin had not let go of Steven's sleeve and could feel the tremor from his body as these words sank in.

'But I'm not a spy!'

'Yes, you are, old man, that's exactly what you are! You stole sensitive papers from a government establishment and passed them to an enemy agent who paid you a very substantial sum of money. It's called espionage.'

'But I haven't got the money – it was all your doing – you forced me to do it. I'll tell them what you and your friend made me do.'

'We are the secret service; the authorities will deny our existence. Nobody is going to believe a story like that, it's ludicrous.'

It was ludicrous, Steven could hardly believe it himself. What chance would he have of convincing the police? 'What am I going to do?' wailed Steven.

'You are coming with me,' smiled Robin.

Steven was taken to an office, much like any other, in a block of offices in Marylebone. Rodney greeted them amiably as they entered.

'How's it going?' he asked.

'All good, Steven has agreed to help us, so we need him to sign the Official Secrets Act.'

'OK, Steven, I'm so pleased you've agreed to help us,' began Rodney, 'You don't have to actually sign anything but you do have to agree to be bound by the Act. Understand?'

'No, I don't. I haven't agreed to help you. I don't want to help you. I have a good job, and until you two came into my life I was happy.'

'Too late, now, old chap. You've been recruited! You still have your job, don't worry. Now, let's get on. My name is Bernard Halesworth and my colleague here is William Bartesthorne. They may or may not be our real names. We've been working together in MI5 for five years. We have a number of agent handlers working for us. Nobody knows who they are. Nobody knows who we are. We are invisible, just like you, Steven. You are just like us.

'Now listen very carefully,' began William, taking over from his colleague, 'You are now officially an agent of MI5. What we call an agent handler. It's a permanent post, but it's part time. By that I mean you don't come into the office every day, only when we call you. Often only an hour or two a week. Sometimes a job will entail working twenty-four seven, but that doesn't happen very often. More often, you won't be needed at all, but you must be ready when we do need you. Now this is very important; there can be no connection whatsoever to us, you understand. Only if your life is at risk must you call this number,' said William, handing Steven a slip of paper. 'Note the word and the number. Read, memorise and destroy. Do you understand, Steven, old man?'

'Of course, yes.'

'Welcome to MI5, old man. You are working for His Majesty's Secret Service now.' Bernard slapped Steven's back so hard he nearly knocked him over.

'You do get paid. Did William tell you that? We call it a retainer; it is quite generous.'

Steven had calmed down a little. He contemplated his situation. It was clear that the alternative to helping these frightening men would almost certainly be prison and he could not face that. He had been given coffee and a sticky bun and the atmosphere in the office had become more comfortable. William was talking –

'Sorry, what did you say?'

'Not much more to do at this stage. We will contact you as and when it is necessary. You do not under any circumstances tell anyone about us or what your new job is. That is vitally important. You will receive payment directly into your bank every month. It won't say on your statement where the money has come from. OK, then, off you go.'

'What? I don't understand.'

'You go back to your job and we'll contact you when we have a job for you. OK?'

'I suppose,' said Steven, uncertainly. 'But how will you pay money into my bank, you don't know what it is, or the number.'

'Oh yes we do, old man, we know everything about you.' Bernard smiled.

# 5

Steven left the building and looked about him to think how to get back to his own office. He was not familiar with Marylebone and couldn't think which Underground stations there might be nearby. He stood on a street corner, looking at the unfamiliar street names, feeling lost in his own city.

Just then he spotted a black cab and hailed it.

He was not in the habit of using taxis as he considered them too expensive, but this was an emergency.

Back in his office, Steven sat at his desk staring at a painting of a Cornish coastal scene on the wall. The picture had been a gift from an old friend and looking at it took him back to a happier time.

'Oh! Hello!' exclaimed Lydia as she entered the office with an armful of folders. 'How are you? I was so worried about you.'

Steven looked up from his reverie and smiled at his secretary. 'Hello,' he said, trying to smile, 'I'm OK thanks, just a spot of tummy trouble.'

'You still look a bit peaky. Are you sure you're all right?' asked Lydia, coming over to the big desk, having dropped the pile of folders onto a chair.

'Yes, please don't fuss, I am all right.'

'Can you tell me?'

'It was nothing, really,' he assured her, trying very hard to put on a brave face.

'I'll get you some coffee,' said Lydia, leaving to office.

The next few months of office routine had allowed Steven to calm down and recover from his encounter with MI5. He could hardly believe that he had been recruited by the secret service.

He had heard no more from MI5, and had tried to push it to the back of his mind, but in quiet moments it all came flooding back, making him sweat.

He had looked at his bank statement, and sure enough there were substantial anonymous deposits.

Lydia had been very attentive and they had developed an easy friendship, calling each other by first names while alone. He was grateful for her friendship. He had even taken her to dinner one evening and was now thinking about taking her to a show, or a concert.

He had resumed his lunchtime walks in the park, and was able to enjoy watching the birds. One day while sitting in his usual seat in the park, a familiar figure appeared, coming towards him. A chill ran down Steven's back as William came closer. 'Oh, no,' he thought, as he stood to greet the newcomer.

'Something we need you to do,' said William without preamble. 'Sit down.'

'I feared as much,' said Steven accepting William's handshake.

'Nice here, isn't it?' said William, watching the ducks for a few moments. 'But you'll have to come with me now, to our new place, and we'll tell you what we want you to do.'

William led Steven to his car, an old and ordinary looking SAAB 9000, and drove out of London on the M40 towards Oxford. 'New office,' he said after a few miles.

After driving for an hour, William left the motorway onto a narrow minor road.

They arrived at a collection of buildings protected by big metal gates. William showed his pass and a uniformed security guard ushered them through the gates. A large sign read, *'Chalgrove Airfield, the home of Martin Baker, famously makers of ejector seats.'*

The new base was in fact just a small office, anonymous among several others.

'Handy this you see, we have use of the airfield,' said William, tapping his nose.

They were met by a smiling Bernard who ushered Steven into a small kitchen.

'Good to see you, old man,' said Bernard. 'Has William told you why you are here?'

'No, he's hardly said a word all the way here.'

'He's a miserable sod sometimes. I'm sorry about that. Have a seat. Drink?'

The next few hours were spent explaining to Steven what was required of him. It would entail taking time off from work and Steven was unhappy about that.

'How can I take time off at a moment's notice?' he pleaded.

'We'll arrange for you to have an accident that will put you in hospital for several weeks,' explained William.

'What? Several weeks! You can't do that!' exclaimed Steven.

'We can do anything we like, old man, you should know that by now.'

Steven's head of section, the unsmiling Mr Cartwright was told by an MI5 agent dressed as a policeman that Steven had been involved in an accident. He asked about his next of kin. The messenger couldn't say where Steven had been taken or even if he was alive.

Mr Cartwright called Lydia into his office and asked her to sit.

'Miss Tremont, Lydia, may I call you Lydia,' the big man began, 'I believe you are, what shall we say, quite friendly with Steven Sebworth?'

Lydia, surprised to be called into the big boss's office, was even more surprised that he even knew of her existence, never mind her relationship, if that's what it was, with Steven.

'Yes, we get on well.'

'Mm, as you wish. Anyway Lydia, I'm sorry to tell you that I've just been informed that Mr Sebworth has had what I'm led to believe was a serious accident.'

'Oh God, I feared as much!' blurted Lydia, her hands covering her face. 'Where is he?'

'They couldn't say, but I expect we will hear in due course.' The big man hesitated, 'I'm so sorry, my dear.'

Lydia was distraught. She was in love with Steven, but had never told him. Now she wished she had. Maybe now she never would.


In William and Bernard's secret training facility, to which Steven had been taken, in a car with blacked out windows, things were hotting up. An intensive training programme was well under way.

Steven had never been interested in fitness or sport of any kind, with the result that his training required what Bernard called special measures.

After several weeks of intense physical routines, as well as lengthy sessions on the range, firing a vast variety of guns, Steven was exhausted.

'Come on, old chap, you can't give in now,' coaxed the instructor.

'On your feet, chop chop!' shouted Bernard, as he bounced into the gymnasium.

'I can't, just give me chance to get my breath,' Steven pleaded.

'Sorry, old dear, we have a deadline. Have to get you ready by Saturday when the next lot come in for the course.'

'Come on, I'll be a little easier on you,' said the instructor. 'See that rope? Climb up it if you can.'

Steven had seen the rope and wondered why it was there. Now he knew. He was sure he could not climb it.

'That's good, go on, bit more, get a good grip with your legs as well. You are doing well, old man.' Bernard and the instructor cheered him on mercilessly until, at last Steven could not go any higher. He loosened his grip on the rope and slid down, finishing up in a heap on the floor.

William came into the gym with a tray of coffee. 'How's he doing?' he asked.

'Not marvellous, but I think he'll manage,' said the instructor.

'Give him some coffee, that should help,' said Bernard.

Steven didn't like it when the men discussed him within his hearing. He said nothing, what was the point.

A little while later, after a cup of strong coffee, Steven was beginning to feel better.

'OK. Now, let's get on then, shall we?' announced the instructor. Bernard was grinning.

'No more, I beg you,' wailed Steven. 'I can't take any more.'

'No, I think you're right,' said Bernard, thoughtfully. Then, addressing the instructor, 'I think perhaps he's ready. What do you think?'

The instructor agreed and the two MI5 men nodded to each other.

Having showered and dressed, Steven was led into room that resembled the briefing rooms in films about the war. Its walls were covered with maps. A table at the front, cover with a grey blanket, displayed a variety of small arms.

'Choose a weapon. You've practiced with most of these so you'll no doubt have a favourite. It's important you are comfortable with your gun,' said Bernard.

'I really don't want a gun,' Steven said, hopefully.

'You may not want one, but one day you will, almost certainly, need one. Come on old man, pick one.'

Steven looked at the guns and chose a Smith and Wesson CSX 9mm, a small automatic, with a choice of ten or twelve round magazines. He hefted the gun and was pleased with its weight; not light at a few ounces over a pound unloaded, but nicely balanced. 'I'll have this one,' he said.

'Good choice!' said Bernard, smiling. 'Take care of it. Go and see Roberts, next door, and he'll fix you up with a holster and some ammunition. Make sure you get some practice with the gun, mind. It might have to save your life one day. That gun is accurate up to ten yards or so. Oh, don't lose it.

We'll make you pay for it if you do. They cost about seven hundred dollars in the States, that's a lot of money here. I don't do conversions.'

'That's it for now, we've got work to do.'

'What do you want me to do?' asked Steven anxiously.

'For now, nothing,' said Bernard, 'Be ready, we'll be in touch. Oh, keep up the range time, you can't allow yourself to get sloppy. Roberts will tell you where when you pick up your holster.'

The two men smiled benignly at their new recruit and then at each other. 'He'll be OK,' said Bernard. 'Yes, I think so', agreed William.

'Off you go now. Don't forget to see Roberts. Remember all we've taught you. When you get the call, you will be given the word, so you know it's Kosher. You must drop everything and be ready for action. Oh, I almost forgot, you are four-four-two. Take care.'

Steven could hardly believe what he was hearing. He had expected to be sent on some mission, probably in foreign parts, investigating some situation that a was a threat to the UK. Now he was being dismissed.

He was driven, in an anonymous looking car, to a railway station and given a ticket.

He had no idea where he was, and the journey was a blur. He looked out of the train window but could not see anything familiar.

When the train reached its destination, he got out of his first-class compartment and made his way to the barrier along with twenty or thirty other travellers.

As soon as he had handed his ticket and passed through the barrier, a man in a dark suit approached him; 'Mr. Sebworth?' I have a car for you. Please follow me.'

The car took him all the way to his flat and the driver just nodded before driving off.

Back home at last, Steven flopped down on his sofa.

It had all been too much for him. His mind was in turmoil. He had endured weeks of brutal fitness training and been subjected to lectures on information retrieval and even been taught various disciplines of hand-to-hand combat. He had spent hours in the range, at first trying to hit a tiny target with a .22 pistol, and later with a nine-millimetre automatic.

He had never even handled a gun before, but he had enjoyed target shooting and was surprised how good his targets looked. And now he had a gun of his own, complete with a valid firearms licence. He could hardly believe it. He had asked if he needed a gun cabinet but they had said no, because you need to have your gun with you at all times.

Events of the past few weeks were going round and round in his head and he was feeling very confused and disoriented.

What must he do now? Go back to work and try to act normally? That was going to be very difficult.

# 6

In the few weeks since being sent on his way by his new keepers, Steven had been trying hard to get back into a routine. Lydia had almost been in tears when she saw him coming along the corridor, but managed to control her delight at his return when he called her into his office and asked her what had been happening in his absence.

Things had quickly settled down, and despite the fear that was constantly in his mind, Steven was able to get on with his job.

His section head, Mr Cartwright, had accepted the explanation for his long absence and had welcomed him back to work with uncharacteristic friendliness.

When he took his usual lunchtime walks in the park he barely noticed the ducks and the lake.

Constantly fearing the false friendliness of either William or Bernard telling him of an assignment, he was unable to enjoy his breaks from the office. At least while he was at work, he felt reasonably safe. They surely would not contact him there. But he knew they would come, one day.

Conscious that he was being watched by William and Bernard, Steven had sought out the shooting range that had been recommended. It was hidden away in a farmyard in Hertfordshire, far enough from any habitation for the noise of gunfire to be heard. There were usually two or three other shooters at the range, men who had enjoyed the safe and harmless hobby of target shooting all their lives were grateful for the opportunity to continue, despite the national ban on handguns. Their need to keep the secret was different from Steven's but they had instilled in him the need for caution as soon as he had attended the first time. A friendly competition among them made his practice more enjoyable.

One of the things they did was simulated combat shooting. Various parts of the farmyard were used as targets and the object was to run round them all and shoot a variety of cardboard cutout enemies on the way. It involved reloading one's weapon as quickly as possible. The winner had the privilege of buying a round of drinks in the pub at the end of the day.

The other shooters were impressed with Steven's pistol and wanted to know where he had got it from. 'Friend in the States,' Steven had said.

He had got used to having the gun snugly holstered under his left arm, and felt naked if he forgot to put it on. He convinced himself that the slight bulge in his jacket was not noticeable.

But despite being comfortable with the gun, and his ability to use it, the fear of being forced to undertake some dangerous, even life-threatening mission was eating away at him.

Even as he sat at his desk, he could feel the gun, it was always there, reminding him.

Supposing, he thought, they were to tell him to kill someone. They might, they had given him the gun, what else was it for?

But how could he? 'Oh, God!' He shouted, then looked up anxiously in case he had been heard.

'Did you call, Mr Sebworth?' said Lydia, coming into the office with the day's mail.

'Sorry, Lydia, a moment of frustration got the better of me.'

'Are you all right?'

'Yes, thank you. What have we got today?' replied Steven, trying to speak normally.

Lydia came closer, 'Are you really all right?' she said, softly.

'What do you mean? Of course I'm all right.' He had spoken more sharply than he meant to and Lydia looked hurt.

'Oh, sorry my dear, yes, I am OK. Just a bit stressed.'

'If there's anything I can do . . .'

Not wanting to remind Lydia of his confession, he said no more. He bitterly regretted telling her of his crime.

When lunchtime came, Steven made his way to the park as usual, keeping an eye open for his keepers and anyone that looked like a spy. He had thought of giving up his visits to the park, but it would not make any difference, they would find him, so why give up his one little bit of pleasure.

He sat in his usual spot and kept his head down. Unaware of the sounds of argumentative mallards or the conversations of passers-by, he nodded off and began to daydream.

*He was with a group of heavily armed soldiers dressed in camouflage uniform, walking cautiously inline down a narrow track. Everything was sandy or sand coloured. Ahead was a village, just a scattering of small houses, also sand coloured. Steven was next to last in the line, watching all around for signs of the enemy.*

*The soldier in front of Steven put up his hand; a signal to stop.*

*Then everything went crazy. 'Take cover, take cover!' The leading soldier was shouting. A barrage of small arms fire drowned out anything else he may have said. Steven was lying flat on the ground, his SA80 assault rifle ready. Shadowy figures were approaching from the direction of the village. Steven was afraid.*

'Are you OK?' a voice from somewhere in the distance. Someone was gently shaking him.

'What? What's the matter?' Steven mumbled.

A group of people were standing round Steven while a young woman was looking closely at him with an anxious expression on her face.

'We thought you were having some sort of attack, or maybe a stroke. You were shouting and shaking. Are you all right. Should I call an ambulance?' she said.

Steven struggled to get a grip, and managed to smile at the young woman.

'I'm OK, thanks. I've been ill,' he improvised, 'I think I must have fallen asleep and had a bad dream.'

The dream had been so vivid, it felt more like a memory. Unlikely as it seemed, could they have put him in an actual combat situation during his training, possibly in Afghanistan, and then somehow suppressed the memory afterwards. 'We can do anything,' William had said. Steven was beginning to believe him.

The little group of onlookers dispersed, leaving just the young woman, still looking anxiously at Steven.

'You are very kind. I'll be all right, thank you.'

'Can I get you a cab or something, or I could walk with you. Where do you live?'

'I work near here, I'll be all right, really. It was just a silly dream.'

But the young woman was not easily put off. 'I'll walk you back to your office – it is an office, I take it.' His clothes gave him away.

A few minutes later, outside the ministry offices, Steven thanked the young woman profusely, but she still hovered.

Here, let me give you my card,' said Steven, reaching in his inside jacket pocket. It simply read, *Steven Sebworth, Ministry of Defence.* No telephone number.

'Oh!' gasped the young woman, 'you've got a g-gun!'

She had spotted his shoulder holster, and was looking frightened.

'It's OK, I'm in security. I'm not dangerous,' pleaded Steven, worried about where this might go.

'You gave me a fright. How silly of me,' she was clearly flustered and they were standing outside Steven's office. He couldn't allow anyone to see this little scene.

'Look, why don't I meet you for a coffee or something and I'll explain.'

'Ooh, that would be nice. My name is Amy, what's yours?'

'Steven; do you know the café in the park?'

'Yes, of course.'

'I'll meet you there, tomorrow. Shall we say one o'clock? I must go now though, thanks again.'

'I'll look forward to it, Steven.' She waved and was gone.

'Oh, Lord, now what am I going to do, she saw my gun. My cover is blown. Suppose she talks.' Steven was muttering as he entered the lift to the second floor. The attendant looked closely at him, but said nothing.

Back in his office, Steven sat with his head in his hands, worried sick.

The phone rang and made him jump.

'Hello, yes, what is it?' he answered, forgetting the correct response.

'Who is she, Steven? Be very careful. Get rid of her.'

'What? Is that you, Bernard?'

'Be very careful. We are watching you.' The phone went dead. Steven was shaking.

'Are you all right, Mr Sebworth?' Lydia called, as she entered the office. 'Oh Dear, you aren't are you. You shouldn't have returned to work so soon after your accident. Can I get you anything?'

'No, really, I'm OK. Just leave me alone for now – please.'

But Lydia could not leave him alone. She wanted to help.

'Can you tell me what is troubling you?' she said, leaning close, and stroking Steven's arm.

He looked up at her and took hold of her hand.

'Can I tell you something in absolute confidence? That you will promise never to repeat?'

'Well yes, of course. I promise.'

'Come and sit here.' Steven looked at his secretary, at her pretty face now looking very worried. He decided he could trust her.

'When I was off work – after the accident. Well, there wasn't an accident.'

'What? I don't understand.'

'No, you couldn't.' Steven looked around him at the four walls of the office. Nobody could hear what he was about to say. 'I was recruited by the secret services. There, I've told you. I'm an agent of MI5, Lydia.'

Lydia put both her hands up to her face, her eyes were wide. She could not speak. She pulled her chair even closer and held both of Steven's hands, tightly.

'Of course I won't say a word, to anyone,' she said at last. 'But it's rather exciting, isn't it?'

'No, it certainly is not. I didn't want to get involved with them, but there was nothing I could do. They concocted the story of the accident and took me off somewhere for a training programme. I am now what they call an agent handler. It means I can be called for duty at any time. And I'm terrified. They watch me. I had a funny turn in the park and a young woman helped me. I had a phone call just now, from one of the agents, telling me to be careful and to get rid of the woman. They must have access to all the CCT cameras all over the city. They seem to know my every move.

The telephone rang and Lydia had to answer it, leaving Steven alone with his fears.

'They gave me a gun. Suppose they want me to kill someone.' He was talking to her back; she was writing as she listened to the phone and didn't hear.

Steven was thinking of what Bernard had said on the phone about the girl he had met - get rid of her. He didn't mean - surely not, and now he had told Lydia – Oh God, help me! He cried, silently, in a prayer to a god he was not sure he believed in.

Steven didn't meet the young woman. Bernard had said get rid of her. He didn't know what that meant, but hoped just not seeing her was sufficient. No doubt Bernard would be in touch again.

# 7

Months went by. Steven and Lydia had been out together a few times, discovering a mutual love of Opera and Ballet. And they had eaten in some of the exotic restaurants in Soho.

Nothing had been heard from MI5. Steven had pushed to the back of his mind the whole agent business.

Then one morning, the phone rang. One word – the word Steven feared. It didn't require a response. He felt a cold shiver down his back, his brow broke out in a sweat.

Quickly making his excuse to Lydia, he left the office, ignoring colleagues he passed in the corridor.

It had been impressed upon him that when the call came, he must go immediately to the meeting place, where he would be told what he must do.

He was acting like an automaton. He dared not think. He just had to get to the place they had told him.

The building looked deserted. Windows were dirty and many of them were broken. There was nobody about. Steven pushed open the door and stepped inside. It was dark and quiet. He hesitated, then moved slowly towards a closed door. He knocked.

'Come in!' came a voice from within. Expecting to see either William or Bernard, he was surprised to see a man he had never seen before, sitting at a large desk.

'Come in, Four-four-two, shut the door. Have a seat. My name is Eleven, I'm in charge of this one.'

Steven sat.

'Now, I don't suppose they have told you anything – no, well I'll tell you. Don't take notes.'

Eleven went on to explain to Steven what the job was and what his part in it would be.

Half an hour later, Eleven stood, shook Steven's hand and wished him luck.

Desperately trying to remember everything Eleven had said, Steven returned to his office, where he quickly scribbled the details of his assignment.

He didn't have to shoot anyone. That was a relief, and it didn't seem too risky a task. Just observation really, but necessary to keep out of sight.

Lydia could see that Steven was anxious about something and hovered about his desk, tidying papers. 'Are you all right, Steven?' she asked at last.

'Well, yes, I can't say anything – you understand.'

Lydia was quick to realise that it was to do with his involvement with the secret services. 'Oh, goodness, of course. Can I get you a drink?'

'What does it mean, Steven?' she asked tentatively when she brought in cups and a cafetière, placing the tray as gently as she could onto Steven's tidy desk.

'I can't tell you. You know that. It will be all right. Thanks for the coffee, haven't we any biscuits?'

'Oh, sorry,' said Lydia, flustered. 'Yes, I'll get some.'

# 8

The premises Steven had been instructed to observe were in a little-known, small fishing port on the south coast, a place he had never heard of; but then, he didn't know the well-known places the

Portslade by Sea, originally the second-century Roman town of Novus Portus, turned out to be very interesting and attractive. Its busy port was a revelation to Steven. He was able to find a room in a back street B&B, away from the shops and places where tourists might gather.

He wouldn't be spending much time in the little back room but it was nice to have somewhere to go home to. Mrs Morgan, the landlady was pleasant and the generous breakfast was sufficient to keep him going for most of the day.

The first few days he spent getting to know the place; different ways from the port to his digs, in case he needed to get away quickly.

His target was a warehouse, on the waterfront of the River Adur, with access to the water by way of a small landing stage. The building had five floors, each with a door with lifting tackle directly over the water. It was easy to imagine the scene as it would have been centuries earlier, with boats unloading and goods being hauled up to the warehouse floors.

Now, however, all was quiet. From Steven's position on the opposite side of the river, in a cramped space between two stacks of containers, he could see everything that might happen. He made himself as comfortable as possible and prepared for a long wait.

A variety of boats came and went along the river, some of them making several trips. Using his father's wartime Zeiss 8x50 binoculars, Steven could see most of what was happening for more than a hundred yards in either direction. So far nothing suspicious. He hadn't been told to look for anything specific so he didn't know what to look for.

After three days, watching from eight in the morning until it was too dark to see anything in the evening, and having seen nothing, Steven was getting really tired of being a spy. He would have to change tactics.

The next day he decided to investigate the warehouse up close.

It was early, but even so he thought it strange there were so few people about. He thought people who worked in these situations were usually early-birds.

He called to a man who was parking his van what was the best way to get to the other side of the river.

'I'll row you across for the price of a beer,' said the man, with a broad grin.

'You're on, what's that these days, fiver?'

'I'll settle for that, come on, boat's just here.' He jumped out of his cab and pointed to a small rowing boat tied up to the jetty.

A few minutes later, after thanking his boatman and paying for his drink, Steven approached his target cautiously.

He walked all round the building. At the rear, looking like a recent addition, was a metal garage door. At the front, one of the large wooden doors, big enough for lorries, had a smaller door let into it.

He tried the knob. Locked.

'Hey, what you up to?' came a shout. Not too unfriendly, Steven thought.

'Hello, do you work here? I wondered if you had any jobs.'

The man, tall, about thirty, with untidy gingery hair and dressed in oily overalls, looked Steven up and down. Steven had dressed in jeans and a dark cotton shirt under his gilet, that he thought looked workmanlike, but it looked as if the man was not convinced.

'What sort of work, you don't look the sort that would be able to lift a hundredweight bale.'

'Oh, you'd be surprised,' said Steven, laughing.

'Show us then,' the man challenged. 'Pass us that pallet behind you.'

Steven looked at the pallet. It didn't look heavy. He picked it up easily and handed it to the man.

'What about one of those sacks there?' he said, indicating a neat pile of large sacks.

Steven bent to get a grip on the topmost sack. It was difficult to get hold of. He pulled it nearer and put his arms around it. Pulling it off the pile, he managed to stay upright, staggering under the weight, he turned to the man and dumped the sack at his feet.

'Now put it back!' said the man, sounding less friendly.

Putting the sack back was more difficult because he had to lift it from the floor. He managed to get his arms round it and attempted to stand.

He fell backwards and landed with the sack on top of him, completely unable to move.

'The man was laughing. 'Good try, mate, that sack weighs nearly two hundredweight. Over two hundred pounds. My name's 'Arold. What's yours'.

'Steven. Could you get this thing off me?' He hadn't meant to give his real name, but it was too late.

Still laughing at Steven's predicament, Arold lifted the sack with ease and replaced it on the pile. He put out a large hand to help Steven up. 'Fancy a cuppa, Steve?'

'Yes, that would be nice.'

'Arold led Steven into the building, using the small doorway. It was almost completely dark inside and it took Steven a while for his eyes to get used to the gloom. He followed Arold blindly.

It was only when Arold switched on a light that Steve could see they had entered a small area among the stacks of boxes and crates, where the employees evidently had their breaks.

Arold busied himself with the makings of tea for several minutes and then handed Steve a grubby mug.

'There you go, Mate. Best cuppa in town. Biscuit?'

'Thank you, Harold.'

'It's Arold. Don't mench. Nah then. What am I going to do with you?'

'What do you mean?'

'What can you do? You aint very strong so you can't be a dockhand. What's your rithmetics like?'

'Quite good, I think. I can do accounts and stuff like that.'

'Any good at cooking?'

'I can fry an egg.'

'I mean cooking books!' Arold laughed.

Steven laughed uncomfortably.

'Funny eh? But could you do it.'

'I suppose I could, but that would be illegal.'

'It would. But could you do it, or should I say would you do it. If say, I asked nicely?'

'Are you offering me a job as a dodgy accountant?'

'I might be, what do you say?'

'Tell me more.'

'Drink your tea.'

'Are you in a position to offer me employment?' asked Steven with a mouthful of bourbon biscuit.

'You mean am I the boss?'

'Well, yes.'

'As it happens, I am the manager – of this part of the business, so yes, I am.'

'I would like to know more about who I am working for.'

'Strictly on a need-to-know basis. No questions.'

'I see.'

'Think about it over another cup of rosie lee* and a biscuit – free of charge.'

*Rosie lee, rhyming slang for tea

# 9

Steven couldn't believe his luck. A few minutes earlier he had no idea how he was going to find out what was going on, yet here it was, on a plate. Too good to be true probably, but he decided to risk it.

After drinking his second cup of tea and another bourbon biscuit - his favourite, Steven stood up.

'You're on, Arold, if the offer is still there, I'll take it. Book cooker at your service.'

'OK, now listen.' Arold dropped the false accent, the rhyming slang and the jokey pally act. 'Anything and everything you see or hear on these premises or while working for me is strictly confidential. If you say a word, anywhere, I will know, and the consequences are serious. Do you understand?'

'Yes, of course, I understand. Tell me more.'

'On the face of it, this is a legit business, importing goods from the Middle East and Africa. Stuff like textiles, fancy leather goods, spices, carved wooden trinkets. It's a good business, good regular income, reliable people here and abroad. You understand?'

'Yes, it sounds interesting.'

'It can be, but there's more.' He hesitated. 'I'm sticking my neck out now. Can I trust you?'

'I've said you can.'

'OK, well, as I said, there's more to it. You know there are people in the countries that we deal with who would like to live in a country like ours. Some of them can barely make enough money to keep body and soul together. Starving, some of 'em. They can't get visas and whatnot to get here legitimately, you understand, and they don't want to pay the crooks who put people on boats to cross the channel and risk drowning. So what can they do?'

'I don't know,' said Steven.

'That's where we come in. Our people over there can offer employment over here to a select few people. For a modest contribution we bring them over in one of our containers.'

'What's in it for you?' Steven asked, puzzled.

'We give them a job in our organisation, they are legal, we give them papers, they can use the health service, everything. They have to work for us, no questions. Fair, don't you think?'

'So where do I come in?' Steven asked.

'Quite large sums of money come into our organisation one way and another that it's impossible to justify, given the nature of our business. You will find ways of moving the money about, in places the authorities can't find.'

'Money laundering, you mean.'

'If that's what you want to call it.'

'I know nothing about that sort of thing. I don't know how I can help.' Steven was getting very worried. Having ventured into the spider's web, as it were, he was now in danger of being eaten.

'Don't worry. You will be given guidelines. One of my chaps will spend some time with you and show you how things are done,' Arold smiled and patted Steven on his shoulder. 'Now, how about a drink? I need one about this time in the morning. It makes the wait for lunchtime less tiresome.'

Steven managed a laugh. 'It's bit early for me actually . . .'

Arold interrupted. 'Nonsense, what'll it be, I've got most tipples, Scotch whisky, Irish whiskey, bourbon, all that kind of thing, then there's brandy, I've got French, Spanish, German – now then, have you tried Mariacron? No, then that's what we'll have.' He laughed again, thoroughly enjoying Steven's discomfort.

Steven was feeling more and more uncomfortable. He regretted getting involved with this character, and feared he would be in danger if he stayed any longer. He already knew too much.

As the day wore on, with Arold showing Steven the vast variety of goods and talking non-stop about opportunities for making money and frequently offering drinks from his comprehensive collection, Steven was near to panic.

When it was close to six o'clock, Steven saw an opportunity to get away.

'Well, Arold, I guess it must be home time. I'll see you in the morning.'

'Going? Where to? Have you got a little wifey waiting for you?

'Well, no, I am not married.'

'Live on your own, do you?'

'That's right.'

'No girlfriend?'

'Well, there is a girl, in the . . .' He almost said office, and struggled to find words. 'She lives near me; I'll be seeing her this evening.'

'Got a house, have you?'

'Flat actually.'

'Own it, do you?'

'Rented.'

'Nice, is it?'

'It's perfectly adequate.'

'Look, you don't want to be going home every night, where is this flat anyway?'

'Palmers Green, near the Bounds Green underground station. Do you know it?'

'London! Oh no, it's a long way from here. You'd be spending all your free time travelling, and think of the expense. No, you can stay here. There's a nice little apartment – come on, I'll show you.'

Steven felt his stomach turn over. Nevertheless, he followed Arold.

# 10

The apartment was on the third floor of the warehouse and was accessed by a series of steep stairs. The accommodation consisted of two small bedrooms, a living space with several easy chairs, a coffee table, a sideboard with a selection of bottles and a large television. An uncurtained window offered a wonderful view of the river. The kitchen was small but well equipped. Steven was thinking it would cost a lot to rent.

'There you are then, what do you think? Asked Arold.

'It's fine. How much?'

'Wotcher mean, 'ow much?'

'Rent.'

'Oh my, you are a card, no mistake,' said Arold, reverting to his jokey persona. 'It's yours mate. Gratis. Goes with the job.'

Steven felt himself sinking further into the trap.

'Well, do you like it? Better than an hour and a half on the train, back to your lonely little gaff, eh?'

'Yes, but I was thinking about a B&B where I could get breakfast and maybe an evening meal. I don't want to have to buy food and cook.'

'No need, all meals are provided onsite! All included in your pay. Marvellous, eh? We look after our people. We are wonderful employers.' Arold was smiling, but Steven sensed a touch of menace. What had he got himself into?

Arold was talking again but Steven was not listening.

'Sorry, what did you say?'

'I said have you got any belongings, spare clothes and stuff?'

'Actually, I did find a B&B and I left my stuff there. I'll go and fetch it.'

'I'll get one of the lads to get it for you, no problem,' said Arold, still with that unpleasant smile. 'What's the address?'

'I can't remember – I will be able to find it though. I'll go now and be back in no time.'

'I'll drive you, just point me in the right direction.'

Steven had no choice but to agree. He followed Arold down the stairs and into a garage at the rear of the warehouse, where a large black American car was the only occupant.

'OK, which way?' asked Arold as he eased the big car onto the road.

Steven had to direct Arold to his B&B. All the time thinking desperately how he could get away.

'Hello, Mr Sebworth, I don't normally allow guests in during the day,' said Mrs Morgan, when he knocked on the door. 'You'd better come in, as you're here.'

'I'm sorry, I have a change of plan, and need to go. I'll pay you for the whole week, but I need to get my things.' Then, leaning close, he whispered, 'Is there a back way out?'

Mrs Morgan was looking very stern and Steven wondered if she would help him.

'Well yes, of course, but why would you want to know about the back way?'

'Just show me where it is when I've collected my bag from my room. OK? Thank you, Mrs Morgan. Here's two hundred pounds.' It wasn't quite enough but Steven felt sure Mrs Morgan would accept it. She wouldn't have to cook or do his laundry.

As quickly as he could, Steven collected his bag and followed Mrs Morgan through the kitchen to the back door. Thanking her profusely, he left, anxiously looking round in case Arold had guessed his intention. All seemed clear.

The rear of the B&B gave onto a narrow lane, overgrown on both sides with bushes and trees. Steven felt safe – for the moment.

Not knowing where he was going, his only thought was to get as far away as possible. By now, Arold must have guessed he had got away, and he would be on his trail in no time.

The lane reached a T junction and Steven had no idea which way to go. But then he spotted a telephone box. He had been told not to use the number he had been given unless it was an emergency. This was.

Steven nervously dialled the number and watched all around for signs of the black car. He was shaking when the phone connected.

'Hello, it's four-four-two here. I'm in trouble.'

'Where are you, four-four-two?

'Portslade on Sea. Lowcliffe Road. Please help me.'

'Stay where you are if it's safe. Help will be with you asap.'

Steven looked at the now silent handset. Could he safely stay where he was? Arold would be looking for him.

Stepping out of the box he looked around for somewhere to hide.

The best hiding place he could find was an ally between two houses, where a collection of various coloured recycling bins gave him cover. He could still see the road and the telephone box. But how would he know if a car arrived if it was Arold or one of the good guys?

While he was pondering this tricky problem, he was startled by a hand on his shoulder.

'OK, four-four-two? Let's go,' said the owner of the hand. Steven almost feinted with relief and the sudden realisation that he was safe.

He scrambled into the snug leather seat of an Alfa Romeo Quadrifoglio. Only then did his rescuer introduce himself.

'Hi, four-four-two, I'm three-seven-oh, pleased to meet you.' He offered his hand at the same time as starting the car and taking off like a rocket, pushing Steven firmly into his seat.

'Good to meet you, too, three-seven-oh,' said Steven, still breathless after the frenetic last few minutes. 'Thank you for being so quick.'

'Do you want to tell me about it? It must have been serious for you to call the number.'

'I really believed I was in a life-threatening situation. How come you were so quick?'

'You won't like this – I've been assigned to keep an eye on you. In case you got in difficulty. Your first assignment. Next time you'll be on your own.'

'I see.'

'No, you get the impression the department is pretty careless about operatives like us, but they do care. You are valuable to them. And it wouldn't do for you to foul up on your first outing. It was the same for me, and I did mess up, big time.'

'How long have you been an agent?'

'Year or so now, I'm just about getting used to it.'

A series of bends commanded three-seven-oh's attention and Steven was able to relax a little. But he could not imagine ever getting used to fearing for his life.

Neither man spoke for a while. The sound of the car's V-six engine was soporific and Steven began to feel sleepy.

Steven was feeling better by the time three-seven-oh drove up to the entrance to the department's new headquarters.

# 11

Hello, four-four-two, back so soon?' William was grinning as he slapped Steven on his back. 'Had a spot of bother, I understand.'

'Well, yes, I'm sorry.'

'Don't apologise, old man. You got out in one piece. That's the main thing, wouldn't you say? Drink?'

'What? Thanks, yes, I could do with something.'

William handed him a generously filled glass and smiled. Steven sniffed the drink. Single malt, he thought. He was not a connoisseur, unlike his father, who had been able to identify most malts just by smelling them. The drink had made him think about his father and he was not listening to William.

'Tell me all about it,' William was saying, 'I shall need a written report of course, but best to get it off your chest while it's still fresh, eh?'

'Yes, of course,' he said, hoping that was an appropriate response.

'Best start from the beginning,' coaxed William.

Steven related his experiences as best he could, and William listened intently.'

'You have done incredibly well! We've been trying to find out what they're up to for ages. We thought it was something along the lines you describe of course, but we had no way of getting the facts. You cracked it! That's absolutely wonderful. I'm sure Bernard will be pleased.' He poured another whisky for Steven and a small one for himself. 'you've still got your gun?'

'Yes, I was afraid they would spot it, and then of course I would have been in trouble, but for some reason they didn't see it. I wished I didn't have it, actually.'

'Don't say that. It's your best friend. Sometimes your only friend. Get you out of all sorts of scrapes. You hang on to it.'

'How come three-seven-oh didn't investigate the warehouse, as he was on the spot, as it were?'

'He was assigned to keep tabs on you, as it was your first job. He has a roving commission, go anywhere, any time. Don't take it as an insult, we always watch first timers. But you did well.'

'I messed up, had to call for help.'

'Look, we know we are sending you into dangerous situations, the phone number is there to be used if needed. It's OK, really.'

Now that Steven was one of the team, both William and Bernard had been very friendly and encouraging. Steven sipped his drink and said nothing for several minutes. William watched him with a paternal smile on his rugged face.

While Steven was wondering what would happen next, Bernard bounced into the room. Whenever he was in a room, his size and personality made it feel crowded.

'Just heard, four-four-two! Well done, old man, well done!' He slapped Steven's back enthusiastically. 'Got another little job for you, OK?'

'Don't you think we should give him a rest, Bernard?' said William.

'No, strike while the iron is hot, while his blood is up, don't you know?'

'I would like a bit of a break,' said Steven, quietly.

'Few days, Bernard, give the man a breather,' pleaded William.

'OK, three days then. What is it today, Thursday? See you Monday morning then, four-four-two. Bright and early. And I'll tell you what we want you to do.'

Steven wrote up his notes and handed them to Bernard, and was given permission to leave.

'Not a word to anyone, four-four-two. Remember? Bye now!'

Steven had no idea how to get home. There was no sign of the little Alfa. He walked to the perimeter of the airfield from where he could see houses. He headed towards them and found himself in a small village.

He spotted a newsagent and went in.

'Good afternoon, I wonder, do you have a bus or train timetable?'

'Used to be a railway-line not far from here but trains stopped runnin' when that chap Beeching did his dirty work, but we do have buses. I think they go most places.' The shopkeeper rummaged under the counter and came up with a booklet that looked as if it had been used as a fly swat. 'Twentypence,' he said, handing the document over.

Steven thanked the man and went outside. Leaning against a wall, he studied the timetables.

There were buses, and they did go to most local places it seemed, but only one went as far as London. It left at six fifty from the town centre and returned at eleven forty-five. For anyone wanting to go to a show, Steven guessed, but not for him. The best option would be to take the bus to Oxford and then catch a train to London.

Just over two and a half l hours later, the train arrived at Marylebone station.  It had made good time.

Still not sure how to get home, even in his home city, Steven asked a man in uniform who happened to be conversant with the Underground system and was pleased to help. He gave Steven detailed instructions.

The journey involved a change of trains and some walking so it was nearly an hour later when he arrived at his home station.

Home at last, he was exhausted and flopped onto his sofa where he fell asleep almost immediately.

The sun was well up by the time Steven surfaced. He drank a cup of instant coffee and ate a piece of toast. He thought again about being an agent. He was not happy. Was there any way he could get out of it? William had said no. Once you're in, that's it.

If they already had another assignment for him, how was he going to explain to Mr Cartwright when he took more time off. He feared losing his job. Not that it was important to him – it wasn't, he hated it. He could get another job, so why was he sorry he might lose it. He realised that it wasn't the job, it was Lydia. He would miss Lydia!

The realisation that his feelings for Lydia were the reason he would be sorry to lose his job, was a shock. He had never been in love before – not even a teenage crush, so he hadn't recognised the symptoms. He thought about it. He felt happy when he was with her and a sort of emptiness when away from her. He had confided in her when expressly forbidden to tell anyone what he was doing, he trusted her. And of course, he thought she was the most beautiful woman he had ever seen. The classic love blindness he had heard about. But she really was beautiful, wasn't she? It wasn't just his love distorted vision.

What was he going to do about it? He would have to tell her how he felt. Supposing she doesn't feel the same. Why should she? He didn't see himself as an attractive man. He looked at himself in the mirror, quite tall at five foot eleven, slim - he only weighed eleven and half stone, light brown hair in no particular style, clean shaven, light blue eyes. No, nothing that would attract a woman he thought. But she had been attentive, and was interested in what he was doing. How to tell her. Thoughts whirled round in his head until he felt dizzy.

# 12

Monday morning. Wondering what happened to the weekend, Steven checked his emails. A coded message that took him ten minutes to decipher told him to go to Chalgrove to meet with William and Bernard.

As he made his way to the meeting with his masters, he realised with surprise that he wasn't worried about another assignment; in fact he looked forward to it. 'I'm MI5, I can do it,' he said to himself, smiling as he entered the Underground station.

Bernard and William were surprised at Steven's new attitude when he arrived at Chalgrove. They looked at each other and shrugged.

'Good morning, old man,' said William, 'had a good weekend?'

'Good enough, thanks. How about you?'

'We've been busy all weekend. We've got a big problem and we hope you'll be able to help.'

'OK, what is it?'

Bernard stood up, 'It has come to our notice that an assassination attempt will be made on an important member of the government. We don't have any details, but the information comes from a reliable source. We need to find out who the target is, who is behind it and where the attempt will be made.

'That sounds a bit too much for me to do,' said Steven.

'Don't worry, you will be just one of many agents working on it. We hope between you all we will be able to nip it in the bud, as it were.'

'I see,' said Steven, not seeing at all. 'Where do I start? I mean, do you have anything to go on?'

'We've divided London into sectors. Each agent will have an area easily workable by one man. This time you will be in constant touch with base – that's us, and as soon as you find anything useful you will contact us – understand?'

'Yes, I think so. So where will I be working?'

'We want you to frequent as many pubs and bars as possible – all expenses paid. Get a little drunk, talk to the people, listen to what they are saying. Sooner or later, someone will say something about the plan. It's too big and exciting to keep information like that to oneself.'

'I see what you mean. I can do that, although I don't normally drink very much.'

'You don't need to drink a lot, make a pint last, but if you think you're on to something it wouldn't hurt to get a bit tipsy, shall we say!' He laughed.

William chipped in, 'Don't overdo it, old man, just a little merry, OK?'

'Yes, of course,' said Steven.

'Now, here's all the information,' said William, handing Steven a box file. 'Study it carefully, and when you're ready, get to work. Don't take too long over it, this is urgent. Keep us in the picture by radio – all the equipment is there. OK?'

'Yes. OK. Thanks.'

'Oh, and take your gun. It's your best friend. Keep it well concealed.' cautioned Bernard.

Once more he had embarked upon the tedious journey home. The bus to Oxford had already taken nearly an hour and he faced a further hour and a half on the train. Then from Marylebone to home, even longer. 'Why on earth did they want to have an office out in the sticks? I'm going to need a car if I'm to do a lot of this,' he mused, as he settled in to an almost empty carriage.

As there was nobody sitting close enough to see what he was doing, he opened the box file and began to study its contents.

Details of the area he was to work in and a lot of stuff about known terrorist groups, and a substantial sum of money in small notes, 'beer money' he smiled. Also, in a metal case was a very small radio transceiver. A neat bit of kit, he thought, one which would need to be kept well hidden.

After a while, he closed the box securely and tried to relax by looking out of the window.

By the time he finally reached his flat in Elvendon Road, Steven had convinced himself of the need to buy a car, even though driving in London was a nightmare, it would be preferable to public transport, especially if he was to take this agent business seriously. He had learned to drive in his father's Golf and always carried his driving licence in his wallet. He had owned an elderly Renault 30 for a while, and he often hired a car when on holiday, but up to now he hadn't really thought of himself as a motorist. He now looked forward to shopping for a car in one of the many dealerships near his home and in the city. He didn't know yet what sort of car it would be, but it would be fun browsing.

For now, though, he had work to do. He had been given a sector of Soho in which to put his ear to the ground to listen for talk of an assassination.

Bernard and William had done their homework; they knew he was familiar with Soho, and in particular the area around Berwick Street and its famous historic market.

Early the next morning he set out once more for Bounds Green Underground station.

He had decided on beige cargo pants and a thick dark blue cotton shirt and a blue padded gilet which effectively concealed his holstered gun. He had on his well-worn Veldschoen because he would be on his feet a lot and they were very comfortable. Seeing his reflection in the underground train window he was satisfied with his appearance. He would not attract any attention.

Berwick Street market had changed since he knew it; now it was mainly fruit and vegetable stalls and fast-food outlets from all over the world. He missed the bric-a-brac stalls, laden with all manner of worthless treasures, and the carpet sellers and the colourful cockneys loudly touting their wares, but for all that, the place still retained its feeling and the people looked happy going about their business.

A good place to start would be the Blue Posts on the corner of Broadwick Street. He wondered if they still did sausage sandwiches for breakfast.

To his delight Steven discovered that they did indeed still do sausage sandwiches. One of those and a large cup of black coffee would see him through to lunchtime at least.

# 13

Where to start? Having enjoyed his breakfast, Steven set about his task without much idea how. He'd kept his eyes and ears alert in the pub but hadn't heard anyone talking about an assassination.

The market was getting busy and sounds of vendors offering bargains filled the air. Women, keen to find the best fruit and veg were prodding and feeling, and stallholders were protesting. It was all part of the game. Steven was fascinated.

'You squeeze 'em, you buys 'em!' shouted a man with a stall laden with boxes of peaches and nectarines, as a woman continued to handle the fruit.

'I'll have a dozen of each, they ain't too bad.'

'Best price in the market, Lady. Twenty pence apiece,' said the man.

'I know, I've checked. Ere, there's a fiver.'

'Thank you, Lady,' said the stallholder, passing over a box of fruit, 'and there's a couple more in there to make it a fiver's worth.'

Transactions like that were going on everywhere Steven looked. There weren't any suspicious looking characters. Time to move on.

He made his way to Carnaby Street, home of trendy fashion boutiques. A group of street musicians were attracting a sizeable crowd; Steven joined them.

The band was quite good, and when a girl came round the crowd with a hat she did quite well. Steven gave her a pound. She smiled.

Steven didn't know what to do. He then noticed a hairdresser's shop. People talk while they're having their hair cut. He went in.

Three men were receiving the attention of their respective barbers and several men were waiting. Steven sat on one of the leather seats in the waiting area. There was a pile of magazines on the next chair; Steven shuffled through them. To his surprize they were recent copies and some were upmarket glossies. He chose a motoring magazine and pretended to read it while listening to the conversations.

'Ave you 'erd about the plot to kill the King?' whispered the small man sitting next to Steven. He could hardly believe he'd hit the jackpot so soon.

'No, not Charlie surely? Where did you hear that?'

'It's goin' rahnd, Guv. They're goin' to do im at the match. You see if they don't.'

'What match? I haven't heard anything about it.'

'Where 'ave you bin idin', Guv, the cup final o' course. His Maj 'll be there won't 'e?'

'But that's terrible. I thought people liked the King.'

'They do, that's why these terrorists want to do 'im in. Oh, that's my turn, Seeya!' The little man took his place in one of the barbers' chairs and was enveloped in a colourful gown.

Unlikely as it sounded, Steven wondered if this could be true. He waited for his turn.

'Who's next?' called a barber with an empty chair.

Steven looked round. 'Me, I think.' He took his seat.

'How would you like it, Sir?'

'Oh, just tidy it up a bit,' said Steven.

'Not seen you here before, Sir. New to the area, are you?'

'Just visiting.'

'How did you come to hear of us?'

'I didn't. Pure chance.'

'Business trip, is it?'

The barber chatted away while he snipped, and Steven hardly needed to reply.

'The man I was sitting next to said something disturbing,' Steven ventured.

'Oh, what was that?'

'He said there was a plot to kill the King! Preposterous don't you think?'

'I have heard talk, Sir. I hope it is just talk. But you can never tell these days.'

'You have? Goodness. But the authorities must be aware, surely.'

'Oh yes, rest assured, Sir. If there's anything in it, they'll know. Now then, how's that for you, anything on it?' He waved a mirror to show the back of Steven's head and brandished a spray bottle.

'That's fine, thank you very much.'

'Pay at the desk, if you would - Who's next?'

Steven was dismissed and the next man took his place, while a young lad swept up the cuttings from round the chair.

'That'll be twenty pounds then, Sir, and if you want to leave a tip, I assure you it will go to your hairdresser.' The young lady smiled.

Twenty pounds! thought Steven, and a tip, I suppose. He reluctantly parted with twenty-five pounds, but then felt better when he remembered he'd been given plenty of money for expenses.

He left the shop and walked further along the street, idly looking in windows full of outlandish clothes.

Could the plot really be to kill the King? Surely there were plenty of politicians more deserving of being bumped off. Steven couldn't think of any politician important enough to merit such a fuss.

MI5 were aware of talk on the street, and if it really was the King, it would explain the size of the operation. It was Steven's and many other agents job to find out who was behind the plot.

# 14

With a renewed sense of purpose, Steven thought where next to go.

I need to get into conversation with some local lowlife, they always know what's happening, thought Steven. Any East End pub would do. Soho was too cosmopolitan. He needed to talk to native Londoners.

He took the Underground to Bethnal Green. It would be as good a place to start as any.

Having visited a number of pubs and drunk a lot more beer than he was used to, Steven was feeling somewhat inebriated. He had managed to get into conversation with a good number of men from whom he would normally keep away, but he had learned no more details of the planned regicide. It did seem certain that an attempt was going to be made however, and the cup final stadium was the likely venue, but nobody had suggested who might be behind the plot.

A little unsteady on his feet, Steven bumped into a man of middle eastern appearance and caused him to spill his beer.

'Ere, oo you shovin'? growled the man.

'Sorry, Mate, someone pushed me,' said Steven, meekly. 'Let me buy you another drink,' Steven spluttered, horrified by the angry looks he was getting, not only from the man he'd bumped but also his three companions, all of whom looked to Steven like Arabs.

'Watch where you're going, you bastard!' breathed the man, quietly and menacingly, as he poked Steven in the chest. 'What you got there?' he said, feeling Steven's gilet. 'Funny sort of gear init?' The other men crowded round.

'E's a country toff, I reckon,' said the first man. 'Wiv 'is funny clothes. What 'ave you got 'idin' under there then? Let's see.' He felt inside Steven's gilet and exclaimed, 'My gawd, 'e's got a shooter!' He grabbed Steven's arms and pushed him against the bar. 'You a cop?'

'No, no, I er . . .'

'What are you, then. Let's see, get 'im in the carsy, guys.' It seemed strange to hear the vernacular from men who were clearly not indigenous.

The men bustled Steven into the Gents' toilet, which was close to where they had been standing.

'Nah then, let's have a butchers,' said the man whose drink Steven had spilled. He pulled the gilet open, revealing the under-arm holster and pulled out the pistol, hefting it in his hand and showing his companions.

'Nice,' said the man. Smiff an Weston, init?'

'Smith and Wesson, actually,' said Steven, unable to resist correcting the man.

'Awright, clever clogs. So, what are you doing carrying a gun? You know it's illegal in this country.' His tone was menacing and Steven was suddenly sober and trembling.

'I was advised that London was dangerous and a gun would be a good idea,' he muttered.

'Oh, London's dangerous!' he laughed, and the other men joined in.

'Tis nah!'

'Can I 'ave 'is gun, Ali?' pleaded one of the men.

'No, you bloody can't 'ave 'is gun, I'm 'avin' it.' Ali was waving the gun dangerously and Steven was afraid he might accidentally pull the trigger.

'Take yer 'olster off!' said Ali. 'And you shut up, you little twerp, Dilwar, or I'll dop you one.'

Steven unbuckled the holster and handed it to Ali.

'Nice bit of kit. 'Elp me put it on.' He removed his jacket and stood with his back to Steven as he strapped the holster on.

'I've always wanted one of these,' he said, placing the pistol in the holster. He replaced his jacket and patted his under arm. 'Neat 'init?' he said turning to his companions. 'You'd never know, would you? What we going to do with this piece of shit?'

'Duff 'im up a bit and leave 'im in the cubicle,' suggested one of the men.

'Anwar, my little Pakistani errand boy, for once, you've said something sensible,' said Ali, giving Steven a vicious punch to his kidneys.

Steven gasped with pain and slumped against the washbasins. Then Ali punched him in the face, drawing blood. Then again, and again. Steven slid to the floor. The other men joined in, kicking him in the ribs, and when he curled up, they kicked his head and back.

Just then a large man, dressed in biker gear came into the toilet.

'What the hell's going on here?' The kicking stopped. The biker kneeled down to Steven.

'Are you OK?' he said, trying to sit Steven up. He turned to Steven's assailants. 'What's this all about?' They said nothing. Faced with a superior opponent they were helpless. But Dilwar faced up to the biker. 'What's it to you?' he said.

'Shut up you idiot!' said Ali, 'I've told you before. I do the talking.'

The toilet door crashed open and two more large bikers came in. 'What's happening, Nigel? Are we having a party?' said a man with a beard and a beer belly.

'Sort of, I guess. These Pakkies have been beating up our little friend here. I was just wondering what to do with them.'

'Well, what are we waiting for?' said another man.

The first man, Nigel, hit Ali so hard that he fell senseless to the floor, leaving an even fight of three against three.

The fight didn't last long. All four of Steven's attackers lay in bloody heaps on the floor. Nigel helped Steven to his feet.

'He's got my gun,' said Steven weakly.

'What, your gun? Who?'

'The one you hit first. He took my pistol and the holster. Can you get it off him please?'

'Why did you have a gun?' asked Nigel reasonably.

'Can we not go into that just now. Get it please.'

'Just as you say, Squire, this one, you say?' he said, nudging the unconscious Ali.

Once Steven had replaced his holster and gun, he felt better. 'Thank you very much, and thank you for rescuing me. I thought they were going to kill me.'

'No problem, I'm sure. Now, shall we repair to the bar and have ourselves a nice little drink? Come on chaps, our little friend needs some restoration.'

Although Steven was slightly built, he had never thought of himself as little, although compared to these new friends, he felt tiny. He allowed himself to be escorted back into the bar, where nobody seemed aware of what had happened.

Nigel looked closely at Steven and suggested he visit A and E to get patched up.

'No, really, I'll be OK,' protested Steven. Let me have a coffee and I'll survive.'

'Coffee for the casualty, and a drop of something in it, please, Barman,' Nigel called, loudly.

Nigel let Steven drink his fortified coffee in silence, watching him carefully for signs of severe injury.

When Steven looked up from his drink, he saw three large bikers smiling at him. He could hardly believe his good fortune. And such unlikely benefactors.

'I think we should get you home. I don't think you've got any injuries to worry about. You are going to be very sore for a few days, but you'll be OK. What do you think, guys?' The others agreed and Nigel asked Steve if he had ever ridden pillion.

Outside, three powerful looking motorcycles were lined up at the curb.

'Where do you live, my friend?' asked Nigel.

'OK, let's go, hop on, hold tight!'

Nigel had experienced degrees of fear in the last few months but nothing like this. Holding on as tightly as he could, he crouched down behind Nigel, out of the wind.

The sound of Nigel's bike. Augmented by the sound of the other two, riding close, was awesome, and by the time they reached Steven's home, he was almost deaf.

The three men insisted on seeing Steven safely inside and they made his tiny living room feel very cramped.

'I feel we should perhaps explain ourselves,' began Nigel. 'This is Andy, and John. I'm Nigel, as you'll have ascertained. We are all doctors at St Bartholomew's Hospital, you'll have heard of it, no doubt. But in our spare time we are bikers. And if we come across incidents like today's, we like to intervene. It's fun, and a relief from the work we do in the hospital. I suppose you could call us vigilantes.'

He beamed at Steven, whose jaw had dropped open.

'Now, I think it fair for you to explain why you carry a gun.' Nigel smiled, but it was clear he was serious. He needed an answer.

Whatever happens, you must never admit who you are working for, Steven had been told. What could he do? Sensing that these men could be valuable allies, he decided to break cover.

'I'm a government agent. I'll probably be shot for telling you, but I have to thank you, and I believe you will not tell anyone, not even the police.'

'Well, well, how exciting. What about that, chaps, a real-life James Bond!'

'Well hardly!' said Steven.

'So, what are you working on, can you tell us?'

'I think I can. There's a plot to kill the King. I'm trying to find out who is behind it.'

'Good grief, so it's true. We've heard the rumours of course, but we didn't believe them.'

'I fear they are true, and I've no idea who is behind it. Or where they plan to do the dirty deed. Favourite is the cup final at Wembley. The King will be there, and although he has been told of the plot, he insists on going. He says the nation needs to see him there.'

'We'll do all we can to help,' said Nigel, turning to his friends for their agreement. They nodded, 'Of course, whatever we can,' said Andy.

'That's great, thanks, Guys.'

'No, Bart's!' joked Nigel.

They all laughed, but stopped when they thought about the threat to the King.

Nigel gave Steven a card. 'That's my mobile number. We're not always available of course, we're kept pretty busy at the hospital, but if you need help and we are free, we will help. That's a promise. Right chaps?'

The other two agreed.

Steven, despite his injuries, felt a warm glow of friendship.

# 15

Time was getting short. The Cup Final was on Saturday and it was Wednesday already. Steven radioed base. None of the teams of secret service men had found out anything.

The big day started with hundreds of plain clothes policemen and many more uniformed men positioned throughout the huge stadium. Even more were outside, on foot and in cars. The majority of the London police and hundreds of men from all branches of the military were ready for anything.

The game, between two of Britain's favourite teams was over. The King was applauded by the huge crowd. And nothing had happened.

But reports were coming in, thick and fast, about incidents all over the capital. Three bombs had exploded at mainline railway stations and more at major shopping centres. Harrods was reported as being in flames and Heathrow airport had been devastated by a whole series of fires.

The awful truth was quickly realised. The threat to the king had been a cleverly organised diversion. While the vast majority of police had been occupied at Wembley, the terrorists had free reign in the capital.

Frequent updates on the number of casualties were broadcast on the radio. Already the total ran into many thousands.

Steven was instructed to report to the London office where he was given the job of studying footage from the numerous security cameras in the city.

'What am I looking for?' Steven asked.

'Faces. The same faces in different locations. If you see the same people involved or just part of the crowd at more than one incident the chances are that they are part of the organisation responsible.'

'Oh, yes, I see. And if I do see such people?'

'Note them and tell us,' said William. 'You can make prints of any frame that looks useful. Just press that button, the machine does it all. Clever, eh?'

It was a daunting task. Hours of video, much of it poor quality, almost all showing scenes of devastation, with damaged buildings and lots of dead and injured people.

Every now and then the camera would show a clear close-up of people. These were the ones to watch carefully.

After watching the videos for several hours, Steven needed a break. He was just about to call to say he was going to get a coffee when he saw a face he recognised, one that he would never forget. The man who had beaten him so viciously.

'William! Bernard!' he called. They came running.

'What have you got?' asked Bernard.

Steven showed the print with the clear image of his attacker. 'I know this guy.'

'Can you put him in more than one incident?'

'Not yet, but I bet I will. He's a villain.'

'Mm. That's as may be, the city is full of villains. It's these particular ones we're after.' William had spoken sharply. Steven, forgetting coffee, returned to his screen.

Some tedious hours later, Steven was almost asleep over the apparatus. He was mechanically scrolling through pages of images. Suddenly he was jerked into full wakefulness. The face he was looking for was there, clear and sharp, and what's more he could identify the location. He called again. 'Are you guys still here? I've got one of them!'

Now that they could place one of the possible culprits the secret service machine was put into top gear. Agents from all over the capital were called in for briefing. Steven was on the little stage with Bernard and William.

All the agents were given photographs of the main suspect, and Steven was put in charge of a unit of four men, all armed.

Six units would keep up a twenty-four-hour surveillance of the Kings Head public house in

Hackney, seven days a week. They would get their man.

Surveillance work is tedious and very tiring. All the men were given ample time for rest and refreshments but they were never far from the target. They all carried communication devices and on receipt of a signal they would converge on the pub in minutes, covering all the exits.

But the best laid plans and all that, aft gang agley. The suspect, one Trevor Banks, was not at the pub. He was not going to be there for a whole week. He was in Brighton with his mother, who was recovering from an operation, He was a good lad, all the neighbours said so. Nobody knew the mother's address.

'Stand down,' Bernard ordered to all the agents. 'Meet at the London HQ soonest.'

'Fat lot of good your info turned out to be, sunshine,' said William, poking Steven in his sore ribs.

'Not my fault he wasn't there,' protested Steven.

'Sorry, just my frustration talking,' admitted William. 'So now what?'

'Resume the surveillance. He'll turn up, you'll see,' said Steven.

'We've nothing else to go on,' said Bernard, cleaning his fingernails with a nasty looking knife. 'OK, let's put the whole thing on again. You're right, Steven, he will turn up.'

And, sure enough, he did, along with a dozen or so rough looking characters, all of them known by sight by Alan Webster, the local detective sergeant who had been seconded to the search because of his knowledge of the area.

'Can you name any of these guys, Sergeant?' William asked.

'Oh, sure, several of them have got form. And they have all been suspects. Some we haven't been able to catch, yet. There's Billy Watson and his kid brother, Albert, Sniffy Harrison, Bruno Trubshaw; I'll write 'em down for you, and I'll get their files. We could bring 'em in for questioning.'

'We could, but not yet. I want to see what they get up to.'

'We don't want another lot of incidents. Surely it would be best to get them locked up,' argued the policeman.

'These are only a few of those responsible for the recent mayhem. If we lock them up the main group will go to ground and we'll never find them.'

'See what you mean, of course,' conceded the DS, and after a thoughtful pause, he added, 'So what are you going to do?'

'At this moment – no idea. Let's get some coffee and then we'll get the chaps together.' William slapped the DS's back, hard.

Our hero, Steven, meanwhile, was just one of the gang tasked with the job of finding the bad guys. He was enjoying the camaraderie. It was something he had never experienced before.

William, energised by coffee, called for a meeting in the briefing room, and the men trooped in.

Now listen up. We didn't get our man this time, but we have identified a number of villains and so we think we're in the right place. The surveillance will continue as before. Any sign of our man and you report immediately, OK? Go to it!'

DS Webster caught William's arm. 'Look, we have already identified some of the local lads, why are we so keen to find this Banks character?'

'We know for sure that Banks was involved, we've got his face on the video, and he was the one that duffed up our man. So, for the time being, he's our number one target. OK?'

William left no opportunity for the detective to respond. He walked off, leaving the policeman feeling inadequate and with a sense that his authority had been taken from him by these bossy secret service men, and he didn't like it. He was used to being the main guy in this area. 'Bloody public-school know-it-alls,' he muttered.

# 16

Blissfully unaware of the hue and cry all around him, Trevor Banks was in deep conversation with three of his cronies over pints of mild and bitter in the bar of the King's Head.

He had been spotted going in a few minutes earlier and the net was tightening. Every exit to the pub was covered. Bernard, with four of his best men entered the pub and approached the bar, a few feet from Trevor's little group. The barman was busy at the far end of the bar so just standing without a drink didn't look strange.

'Oo are they, Trev, never seen them rahnd 'ere before,' said Sniffy Harrison, sniffing.

'Tourists, I reckon, no prob,' assured Trevor.

'Not so sure,' said Bruno, they're looking at us.'

Bernard moved in close, and his men surrounded Trevor's group.

'Ere, what's this?' exclaimed Trevor, suddenly alarmed.

'Trevor Banks, you're under arrest for terrorist activities.

'Not me, Guv, never. Straight as a die, me. Ain't that right, Sniffy? You tell 'em.'

'E ain't no terrorist, Guv'nor. Where'd you get that idea?'

'You, too, Sniffy, come with us,' said Bernard, taking Sniffy's arm. 'You have some questions to answer.'

All four men were hustled out of the pub, protesting loudly. A police van had just arrived and they were all safely locked up inside.

The whole operation had been observed by a little dark man sitting in the corner, unnoticed by Bernard and his men. He went to the telephone on the corner of the bar and spoke briefly. Then, making sure the police had gone, he left, and scuttled off down a nearby alley.

In a quiet suburban semi, a group of men of middle eastern appearance were in deep conversation.

They had heard of the arrest of Banks and Harrison.

'I know these men are only a small part in the operation but they know too much about it. We can't risk the whole thing because of what they might tell the police,' said Mukhtar Ghazni.

'But what can we do? They are locked up,' protested Bashir Bijan, speaking in his native Farsi.

Mohammad and Mohib chipped in with their suggestions and soon they were all talking at once, all in Farsi.

'Enough!' shouted Mukhtar. 'Speak English. We don't want our neighbours to hear foreign languages spoken. I have an idea. Listen, all of you.'

They calmed down to listen to their leader and huddled round him.

Mukhtar spoke for several minutes after which the group broke up and left the house, each with instructions.

Mukhtar Ghazni's little group was only a small part of a very large and widespread organisation known as Shamshir Allah or Sword of Allah, the object of which was to remove all foreign troops from their country and restore Islamic traditions and law. They were known for recruiting local criminals to help them. They paid well.

All known Shamshir Allah's adherents were under constant observation by MI5, and had been for a long time. Up until recently they had been quiet, but MI5 had suspected something was brewing.

Although there was no proof that Shamshir was responsible for the recent disturbances, they had many of the similarities to incidents that had definite Arab involvement.

In the interview room of a small police station in East London, two frightened looking men were being questioned by Bernard and William. Also present were Steven and Chief Inspector Gordon Mackay, there to see fair play.

'We know you were involved in the, what shall we call them, disturbances, what we would like to know is who were you working for?' said Bernard, in friendly manner.

'No, you've got it wrong, Guv. We just got mixed up in the crowd when that bomb went off. People was panicking, ain't that right, Sniffy?' pleaded Banks.

'Aye, we was running from the commotion.'

'We've got you on video, Banks, and you, Sniffy, you were there, and we think you are responsible for at least one of the explosions.'

'You can't prove nothing,' whined Sniffy.

'Why's that, do you think?' said Bernard, softly.

'Cos we was careful . . .'

'You idiot!' shouted Banks.

'Oh, I'm sure you were careful. Tell us about it.'

'For Gawd's sake, Sniffy, shut up. Don't say no more,' Banks pleaded.

'Too late. We've got you on tape, as much as admitting responsibility. OK, sergeant, lock 'em up. We'll talk again later.'

'I'll 'ave you, Sniffy Harrison, you see if I don't, you stupid bastard,' Banks growled, as they were led away to the cells.

# 17

Meanwhile the Sword of Allah had been busy. In a skilful and coordinated series of raids they had captured a number of key men from MI5 and the police. They had acted so swiftly and so silently; nobody had noticed the men were missing until the following day when they failed to turn up for duty.

'God it's hot,' muttered Graham, as he woke, clutching his aching head. 'What's going on? Put the light on somebody.'

A groan from nearby, followed by an exclamation. 'What the hell? Where are we? Is that you, Gray?'

'Yes, Alan? You OK?'

'No, I've got the worst headache I've ever had and I feel sick. Where are we, and why is it so dark?'

'Hello!' someone shouted.

'Who's that?'

'My name is Philips, who are you?'

Before long, ten men had identified each other and begun to piece together what had happened.

'You aren't one of us, are you?' Detective Inspector Alan Davies asked, addressing a man he could not see.

'No, my friends and myself are doctors, from Barts' Hospital. Are you police?'

'Some of us are, some are secret service – MI5 I believe.'

'Do you know what happened? And where we are?' asked John.

'Doctors, did you say? Why are you here?'

'You tell us,' said Nigel.

'Is that the three musketeers from Bart's?' came a feeble voice in the darkness. 'Remember me, Steven, who you rescued from a beating?'

'God, yes, of course! This is incredible,' said Andy. I like the three musketeers; I think we should keep that.' He laughed. 'But how come you're with all these coppers?'

Before long the men had all introduced themselves and they had realised they were all involved in anti-terrorist organisations. They had not been able to identify their location.

'What I can't understand is why you doctors are here,' said the inspector. 'Obviously the terrorists have got us locked up here because we're all working against them, but you doctors . . ?'

'That's easy, when we are off duty, we're a sort of vigilante group, righting wrongs and so on. We got involved in the recent shenanigans, and so the villains thought we were either part of the police or you secret guys.'

'I see, I think,' said the inspector.

'Look, never mind about that, where are we and how are we going to get out?' This was Bernard, who hadn't said anything up to then.

'I guess, from the heat, that we're in the middle east somewhere,' suggested someone.

'That can't be right. It would have taken a long time to get us to the middle east. We couldn't have been unconscious all that time.'

'There are drugs that will put you out for a very long time,' said Andy. 'That is not a problem. We are almost certainly in a terrorist stronghold, probably Afghanistan I would guess.'

'Oh, that's wonderful. What do you think they are going to do with us?' asked Steven.

'I'm pretty sure they aren't going to do us any harm. That wouldn't help them. We are for negotiation purposes. Hostages.' This was the inspector again.

'Has anyone got a light of any kind?' asked a voice.

No one did. Not so long ago a group like this would have including a number of smokers and they would have lighters or matches, but now very few people smoked and not one of them had a light.

The door opened with a bang and the room was suddenly lit with powerful floodlights, so bright the men all covered their eyes. Gradually, as their eyes adapted to the brightness, the men could see their captors. Three men with Kalashnikovs cradled in their arms, stood observing the group with grim expressions. At last, one of the men spoke.

'I see you have introduced each other, and you have guessed why you are here. And you guessed correctly that you are in Afghanistan. Well done, gentlemen. I am impressed. However, it will not do you any good. Your intelligence will not get you out of here, I assure you.

We will be making certain demands of your government. If those demands are met, you will be released. But, if they are not, by the deadline we will set, at the end of one week you will all be beheaded. And the film of your demise will be broadcast on all the television channels of the West. Do you understand?'

There was no reply from the hostages.

'Do you understand?' the man repeated loudly.

'Yes,' said somebody.

'Very well. In a little while you will be fed.'

The men left, leaving the lights on.

'They're going to kill us,' wailed somebody, 'the bastards are going to chop off our bloody heads, Oh God!'

'Enough of that!' said Inspector Davies, sternly. 'I don't expect that sort of talk from my men.'

'Sorry, Guv. Got the better of me.'

'And don't call me Guv. My name is Inspector Davies. If you know me well enough you can call me Alan. Is that understood?'

'Yes, Sir, I mean, Inspector.'

'Now, listen, all of you. I think I am the senior officer here so I'll take charge.'

'One moment, Sir, if you don't mind, I think you'll find I am the senior here. I hold the rank of Commander,' said Bernard, quietly. My name is Bernard Halesworth, Commander in the Royal Navy, seconded to MI5, although in my unit we don't use ranks. There are several of my agents and handlers here. Normally they are forbidden to reveal their involvement with me, but I think it might be permissible for them to say who they are. You can be my second in command, Inspector; that is if there are no other contenders.'

The inspector harrumphed agreement and as there were no other claimants to leadership, it was accepted. The men gathered round the two leaders.

'Right, now we know the score. They can hear us, that's obvious, so we have to speak very quietly. They mean business, and we know they are not bluffing. It's up to us to get out of this because the government will not agree to any deal. We don't know how long we have, but we can assume days rather than weeks.

'Do you have a plan, Sir?' asked a policeman.

'No, I don't, yet.'

'We could jump them,' suggested one of the MI5 agents.

'That would more than likely result in a premature execution. No.'

There was a lot of muttering and grumbling among the men for some minutes, before Bernard called for order.

The lights went out. The men continued to offer suggestions and Bernard rejected them all.

# 18

Several days had elapsed, but in total darkness there was no way of telling day from night or how much time had passed. Bodily function was an indicator but not an accurate one, as in stress conditions the body performs differently.

'Any one got any idea what day it is?' someone asked, not for the first time.

'I know it's dinner time, I'm starving,' said another.

Food had been provided at intervals but Andy was convinced the intervals were irregular and designed to confuse the captives.

'They want to make us think more time has passed than actually has. They gradually reduce the intervals between meals and as there is very little food our hunger is not a help in determining the passage of time. They want us to panic. Thinking that we are going to be killed imminently.

'Devious bastards. I'd like a chance to get my hands on them,' said Philips.

'I'm sure we all would. Is that you, Philips, I thought so, and we probably will. We just have to be patient,' said the inspector.

'So, if you're right about the meals, Doc, how can we measure time accurately?'

'I know all sorts of ways if I'm outside, by the sun and the stars, but in here in total darkness, I admit to being completely stumped.'

'Well, I reckon we've been in here four days,' chipped in the inspector, who had been listening to the conversation.

'Long enough for this lot to contact the authorities with their demands?'

'Probably Inspector, and long enough for our people to be worried about us,' suggested Nigel.

By now, the whole group were listening, and several offered their own theories.

'Look, it doesn't make much difference knowing how long we've been here. What is important is how we are going to get out.'

'Before the bastards chop off our heads!' said one of the agent handlers who had not given his name.

'Precisely!' agreed the inspector. 'Now listen, I have an idea. It's a bit risky, but it might help us to find out where we are, and what sort of security there is.'

'What do you mean, risky?' asked Andy.

'Risky for me. I'm going to try to get out.'

'What, on your own?' asked Bernard, who had been unusually quiet.

'Yes, to begin with.'

'What's your plan?' several men asked at once.

On the whole, the inspector's plan was judged foolish and unlikely to work. Most thought he would just finish up dead.

'Unless anyone has a better idea, I'm going ahead,' said Davies. 'I'm determined.'

'I forbid it, Davies. If you get yourself killed it puts the rest of us at a disadvantage,' said Bernard, sternly.

'It's better than nothing. We can't just wait here for them to kill us,' Davies insisted.

'OK, so when are you doing it?'

Just then the lights went on and the man came in with rush baskets of food.

'Now!' whispered the inspector.

He suddenly jumped up and tackled the food man, sending the baskets flying and the man on the floor. He banged the man's head on the concrete floor several times until he stopped moving.

Another of their captors came running, Kalashnikov at the ready. Davies was ready for him, tripping him and sending him headlong into the group of astonished onlookers, where he was swiftly disarmed.

A squad of uniformed men appeared at the door and fired their guns into the ceiling, bringing down a cloud of plaster and dust. The noise stunned the men for a moment and the soldiers quickly restored order, rounding up the captives into a tight group.

They spoke in Farsi to the second man who had been attacked by the captives. The man who had brought the food was still unconscious.

Inspector Davies was quickly identified as the instigator of the fracas and was handcuffed and led away.

'We will deal with the rest of you later,' said one of the soldiers as they left. Closing the door and putting out the light.

'Fat lot of good that was!' said Andy, 'He'll just get himself killed.'

'I did warn him,' said Bernard. 'Now, listen, I know you all think the inspector's action was folly, and I thought so, too. But I think he knew what he was doing. We shall have to see.'


Inspector Davies was roughly dragged out into an open compound, reminiscent of a bull-ring. Walls of mud brick about ten feet high surrounded the area. At one end was a single storey building, made of the same sandy coloured mud bricks.

In the middle was a pole surrounded by sand stained a darker colour. Davies guessed it was blood, he also guessed that he would soon be adding his own blood to the sand.

His captors said nothing as he was tied securely to the pole. The soldiers left.

'Now what?' thought Davies. 'Are they just going to leave me in the sun without water?'

He had feared that the worst that could happen would be premature beheading, but he was hoping he would just be punished and returned to the group to show them what would happen if they tried anything again. This was not what he had anticipated. The sun was hot. He was already thirsty. He had no head covering.

Some hours later, when the sun had lost a little of its heat, two soldiers appeared. One had an ugly looking lash, something like a cat-o'-nine-tails.

They're not going to behead me, thought Davies. At least not yet. This is going to be tough, but the chances are I'll be returned to the group.

One of the soldiers tore off Davies' shirt and stood back while the other one took his position with the lash. Neither man spoke a word.

The first stroke of the many strands of leather tore skin from Davies' back and almost caused him to lose consciousness, so severe was the pain. The second was worse. He was gasping. The third made him wish they had taken off his head. He had never experienced such agony. The leather thongs had metal teeth embedded in them. His skin was in tatters.

The fourth and fifth lash rendered Davies a bloody mess. He had slumped against his bonds and was drooling, incapable of anything but the sensation of pain.

The soldiers evidently considered they had done enough and left their victim to suffer.

As it began to get dark, it got cold. The vicious stinging of the lashes was slightly diminished by the drop in temperature and Davies was able to stand up, easing himself against the ropes.

It occurred to him that Jesus had suffered such a beating, and he offered a futile prayer.

Now that he was suffering from the cold almost as much as the pain in his back, he tried to get out of his bonds. His blood had made the ropes slippery, and with great effort and almost unbearable pain he managed to get loose.

It was dark in the compound and completely silent. He guessed the small building housed the soldiers and they were probably asleep. Although they would be sure to have a sentry of some kind.

Should he try to scale the wall, or get back to his fellow prisoners. His pain made it difficult to think.

There wouldn't be much point going back, although that had been his intention originally, when he was cooking up this plan.

No, he would try to get out. Maybe he would be able to get help. Slim chance in this hostile country, but worth a try. There were still British troops in Afghanistan, he might be able to contact them.

All this was going round in Davies' head seconds after getting loose. He made for the perimeter wall. It was, as he had judged, about ten feet high. But it was built with rough mud bricks and there were gaps between the bricks. He might be able to climb. But he was weak from his beating and very cold.

Sometimes, when faced with insuperable odds, the human spirit takes over. Davies began to climb.

It was agony, every inch gained caused him excruciating pain. But he made it to the top. Still no sound from the soldiers.

Looking over the wall, Davies could see a dozen or so small mud brick buildings in a roughly circular group. Light was coming from somewhere, probably cooking fires. He dropped down, landing hard but without further injury. A line of washing hung limply from a hook on the side of one of the buildings. A thick shirt attracted Davies's attention. He quickly grabbed it and put on. It was well worn but warm and not too hard on his wounds. The climb had sapped what little energy he'd had left. He sank down to his knees; leaning against a pile of vegetables he fell into a troubled sleep.

When the heat of the sun woke him, he quickly moved away from the houses. His back hurt so badly, he couldn't think. He had no idea which way to go, but he knew he had to get as far as possible from the people who had taken him prisoner. As he staggered along a rough path it was his only thought.

He had to stop frequently to rest but he was determined to get help if he possibly could, whatever the cost to himself.

As the sun rose higher, so did the temperature, but it also revealed the landscape.

In Davies' imagination Afghanistan had been a bleak barren sandy coloured country, full of bearded and cloaked men, desperate to cause mayhem.

What he was seeing was a beautiful landscape, with a wonderful hilltop castle and groves of greenery, people dressed in colourful clothes and happy looking children. How wrong were the television programmes about British soldiers, fighting the Taliban. No doubt the Taliban was a harsh reality, but it was not the whole story.

Eventually, after trekking some considerable distance and exhausted almost to the point of total collapse, he saw a limp Union Flag on a large building.

He staggered to the door and collapsed before he was able to knock. The door opened and a soldier, dressed immaculately in tropical khaki looked aghast at the wretched figure before him.

'My God! What happened to you?' he paused a moment then called, 'Sergeant!' A soldier appeared. 'What do you make of this? Do you think he's one of ours?'

'He's not an Afghan, Sir, looks like a westerner to me. Shall I take him in, let the doc have a look at him?'

'Do that, Sergeant. I'm off now, I'll see you later.'

The sergeant called for a couple of his men and Davies was carried to the medical room.

Captain Angus Ross, of the newly formed Royal Regiment of Scotland, was the unit's doctor, although if asked he would insist he was from the King's Own Scottish Borderers.

He had seen some terrible injuries since being posted to Afghanistan so Davies' lacerated back did not surprise him unduly.

He instructed a nurse to take off Davies' filthy blood-soaked clothes and clean him up. 'He'll be needing water and some nourishment, too, nurse. See to it will you?'

'Sir!' said the nurse, who in turn instructed her team to help.

The nurse, Lieutenant Lucy Preston of the Queen Alexandra's Royal Army Nursing Corps was on her first mission in Afghanistan. She had not so far seen many injuries as bad as these. She offered Davies a cup with a little spout and he was able to drink a little water.

She gently sluiced the worst of the congealed blood from Davies' back and was appalled at the damage that was revealed. Strips of skin hung from his back, leaving long raw areas.

Another nurse brought soup and carefully spooned it into Davies' mouth. He tried to smile his gratitude.

It was quite a while before he was able to speak, and when he could, he made little sense.

'We'll get him to intelligence as soon as we've got him patched up,' said Lucy. 'But now he needs rest. Be careful with him, nurse.

# 19

When Davies had rested and his injuries had been treated and dressed and he had taken a little more soup and an egg, he told the nurse he was ready to explain what had happened to him.

The intelligence officer, a sergeant who would only admit to the name Watson, was questioning Davies.

'Where is this place where the others are imprisoned?'

'I've told you; I don't know.'

'But you found your way from it, so you must know where you came from.'

'I was badly injured. I just got as far from the place as I could. I just walked in the hope I would find some help.'

'Right, so let's retrace your steps. You arrived here, what twenty-four hours ago?'

'I've no idea.'

'Now, Sir, you must help me here. You must know how long you were there.'

'I tell you, I don't know. All I do know is that I somehow managed to get away after I had been severely whipped. I was delirious with pain. I acted purely by instinct.'

'Are you ex-service?'

'I was in the Paras before becoming a policeman. Based at St. Athan, Special Forces Support group. Did fifteen years.'

'That explains a lot,' said Watson. 'A lesser man would have succumbed to injuries like yours.'

'All I could think of was those men in that dark room waiting to be beheaded. I had to get help.'

'Tell me more about that.'

'There were about ten of us, a mixture of police and secret services. Oh, and three doctors.

'What were they doing there?'

'They told us they were a kind of vigilante group, looking for trouble and sorting it out.'

'How extraordinary,' mused the sergeant. 'So how come this mixed bunch got itself abducted?'

'I think it was just random. They were all on the street after the disturbances. You'll not have heard what happened I suppose.'

'We do have radio you know,' said the sergeant, indignantly, 'It's all quite civilised here. Of course I know what's been happening back home. How did they get you?'

'I don't know. I was investigating an incident in which several people had been injured when I was knocked out. I didn't wake up until I found myself in this dark room with the other guys.'

'Then what happened?'

'An Arab with a huge black beard and an ugly looking knife in his belt came in and told us we would be beheaded unless they got what they wanted from the government.'

'And what did they want?'

'They didn't say; just certain demands, or something like that.'

'What do you think they want?'

'They want our forces out of Afghanistan. They want it to be purely Islamic, with Sharia law and everything. Surely you know that. It's their country after all. But how did it all start? Why is the army here at all?'

'If you really want to know,' said the sergeant, looking intently at Davies. 'I'll tell you.'

'Well yes, you know better than most, I guess.'

The sergeant explained that it had all begun when Al Qaeda and the Taliban were blamed for the terror attack of 9/11. 'Osama bin Laden and all that. Britain got involved in 2001 when a coalition of forces led by the United States, including Afghan troops from the Northern Alliance, captured Kabul and Kandahar. After that, seven thousand soldiers remained with a peacekeeping role. But then the Taliban fought back, with terror attacks right through from 2003 to 2006. Are sure you want to hear all this?'

'Of course I do, thank you, Sergeant.'

'Very well. In 2004 the first British soldier was killed. The Taliban deployed IEDs and in 2006 there were thirteen hundred attacks on vehicles.

Camp Bastion was established in Helmand province. A town of forty-thousand people, built from scratch in the desert!'

The sergeant looked again at Davies to see if he was listening. He went on, 'There were six hundred aircraft movements a day. All together there were one hundred and thirty-seven UK bases and nine and a half thousand troops. By 2009 four hundred and fifty-six troops had been killed.

In 2010 a joint operation involving fifteen thousand British, American and Afghan troops drove the Taliban from Helmand. Four-hundred and fifty UK troops remained to train advise and assist.

The whole operation had cost the UK forty billion pounds. The Taliban had killed four thousand Afghan troops.'

'That's appalling,' said Davies, 'do go on,'

'In 2015 British forces redeployed.
That's it really. The Taliban have declared that they will not stop fighting until all foreign troops are removed from the country.'

'Thanks for that history lesson, Sergeant. I didn't know most of that. So, I have to ask – why are we still here.'

'It's a question we all ask almost every day. Ours but to do or die and all that. Nothing changes. The brass-hats and government ministers make decisions that mean death to hundreds of people and it's just talk round a table to them. And, of course the arms manufacturers get rich. The real winners in any war are the guys that make the guns.'

An officer entered the room. 'How's it going, Sergeant? Let me have a report as soon as possible.' He left without another word.

'Sir!' said the sergeant. And in a whisper to the policeman, 'They always want stuff yesterday.'

'Can I go now?' the inspector asked.

'As far as I'm concerned you can, but I don't know about his nibs,' he gestured to the door through which the officer had left.

'Do your best to find those guys, time is running out.'

'Will do, Sir, I will pass on the information you've given me in a matter of minutes.'

'Thanks, Sergeant.'

The inspector's dramatic appearance had caused quite a stir; top officers were discussing the demands the terrorists had made at the same time as trying to establish where the hostages were being held. They didn't have much to go on. Davies' information was not very helpful. He had walked a considerable distance in something of a daze. He had no idea where the hostages were.

It had been Davies' intention to go back himself and try to get the men free, but he had to admit he would have had very little chance on his own and he had no idea where they were anyway. Now he was angry, with himself as well as with the terrorists, but most all he felt frustrated. He banged his fist on the table, startling nurse Lucy, who was keeping an eye on him.

'Are you all right, Sir?' she said, moving closer.

'No, I've let my colleagues down.'

'You clearly did the best you could, and might have been killed in the attempt. You mustn't blame yourself.'

'But I do, don't you see? Yes, I took a risk, but it hasn't helped them.'

'OK, now let's think. I'll make a cup of tea and we'll brainstorm.'

'Mm,' Davies mumbled.

Nurse Lucy returned a few minutes later with tea and biscuits. She smiled at Davies as she sat down beside him. He managed a feeble smile in return.

While they drank their tea and nibbled biscuits, Lucy didn't speak. She was aiming to get Davies to relax. When they had finished the refreshments, she moved closer.

'My name is Lucy, we can't keep using ranks, what's your name?' she began.

'Alan Da - it's Alan.'

'Now, Alan, I want you to describe what you saw when you got out of the compound you told us about.'

'There were some little houses in a rough circle. There was washing hanging from one of them.' He suddenly looked up, 'I stole a shirt!' he laughed at the memory. 'My back was so painful, I had to cover it.'

'Go on, what else did you see?'

'A wonderful castle on top of a hill, and a valley filled with greenery. I'd always thought Afghanistan was barren. But it's beautiful. You know, really beautiful.'

'Yes, I know, I was surprised, too. Go on, you're doing well. What else did you see?'

'There was a railway line. I crossed it. I could hear a train in the distance but I didn't see it. Then I had to cross a small river. I was afraid it might have a strong current and sweep me away, but although the water was moving fast it was quite shallow and easy to wade through.'

'Hold that thought a minute, Alan. I'm going to get a map. I should have thought of that before we started.'

Lucy was only gone a few minutes and when she returned with the map, Alan was bursting to tell her something else he had remembered.

'There was a mosque! Covered in beautiful coloured tiles.'

'Can you describe it?'

'No, but I could draw it!'

Lucy excitedly ran to her office and came back with paper and pencils.

'There. Take your time. Put in as much detail as you can.'

Alan began to draw, tentatively at first but then as he visualised the mosque the drawing developed.

# 20

Armed with Alan's description of his journey and his drawing of the mosque, it had been possible to plot his route on the map and make an educated guess as to the location of the compound where the hostages were being held.

'Well done, Lieutenant!' said Colonel Rogerson when Lucy presented the information. See me when this is all over, we can use a talent for getting information like yours.'

Having identified the terrorists' lair, a raid was being planned. Great care would need to be taken to safeguard the hostages. It would be 'softly softly', the colonel explained.

'The paras will drop in at night and establish a base, here,' the colonel indicated a natural outcrop of rock on the large-scale map. 'It looks big enough to conceal ten men and their equipment. They will be in radio contact with HQ, that's me.' He allowed himself a smile.

'The main group will rendezvous at oh-six-hundred. We will be using non-lethal weapons, you understand, but they can still do a lot of damage, and I don't want any accidents. Regular weapons will be available in the vehicles, just in case. They have GPMGs, HMGs and grenade launchers. But I don't want this to turn into a major conflict. From what we gathered from the police inspector, there are only a few enemy personnel. We must protect the hostages at all times. Stun grenades will be used to incapacitate the bad guys. Then it's just a clean-up operation. Lieutenant Willis, your men ready?'

'Yes, Sir, all set.'

'Who's transport, oh yes of course, Wilson. There are ten hostages. What are you using?'

'Two Mastiff troop carriers, Sir. There will be sixteen men with me; they will come back on foot leaving room for the hostages, and we have an Oshkosh we borrowed from the Yanks as well, Sir,' answered Sergeant Wilson, smartly.

'Oshkosh, Sergeant?' queried the officer.

'Like a Humvee, Sir. Lieutenant Willis will be commanding the unit from that. It's fast and well equipped. He has three men with him as well.'

'Of course. Very good, Sergeant. Carry on.'

Sergeant Wilson was proud of the machines in his command and the heavily armoured Mastiff was his favourite. In it he felt invincible.

'Good. I think we're done. Thank you, gentlemen.'

'Oo does e think e is?' asked Brian Anderson, a private in the main attack group, 'Ruddy Monty?'

'I doubt he's ever seen action. But he seems fair. Treats his men well,' said Dai Jones.

'You would say that, creep.'

'No, be fair, Bri. Give him a chance.'

'No choice, 'ave we?'

'Come on, get our gear together.'

It was getting dark. It gets dark very quickly in hot countries. The little group of paras were boarding a mean looking Chinook helicopter. The men said little at the start of a mission. There was too much to think about.

The colonel's group had longer to prepare. The men were joking and ribbing each other, to take their minds off the mission.

The hostages, still in total darkness apart from brief respite at mealtimes, were increasingly worried about their chances of survival. Their captors had not mentioned beheading again and they were thankful for that, but it was still a real worry. They worried about Inspector Davies. They hoped he had got out somehow. Had he been caught and killed or could he possibly have found help.

Some of the men prayed.

They still argued about how long they had been held in this increasingly smelly dungeon.

There was only the one hole in the floor which served as a toilet, and in darkness it was difficult to aim accurately. The area around the hole was disgusting.

'Why don't we ask them for a mop and bucket and some water,' suggested Andy, one of the doctors. He was worried about infection.

'Worth a try; one of them'll have to clean up after we're gone, so they'll be glad for us to do it.'

'Are you volunteering then?' said somebody.

'I'll take a turn. I think we all should,' said John.

'Watch out, dinner's coming, said Graham.

Two men, holding not the expected baskets of food, but ugly looking Kalashnikovs, came into the room and put on the floodlights. The captives covered their eyes until they were able to stand the glare.

'You come. Now!' shouted one of the soldiers.

'Quick, quick, come now!' said the other one.

The hostages reluctantly got themselves into a rough group and followed the first man out of the door. The second soldier brought up the rear.

'What's happening?' Bernard asked.

'No talking, quick,' said a soldier.

'I demand to know where you are taking us,' said Bernard.

'You soon find out,' said the soldier, sharply.

'Leave it Bernard, old man, don't make 'em cross,' advised one of the men. 'We'll find out soon enough, and if they're taking us to be beheaded, I'd rather not know.'

They were ushered into the large open area that the inspector had likened to a bull-ring, and where he had been flogged. The post had been removed, but the area where it had been was stained with blood.

'You go against wall,' one of the soldiers shouted.

The men looked at each other, thinking they were about to be shot.

'They aren't going to chop our heads off then,' speculated Graham. 'I think I prefer shooting.'

'You keep your ideas to yourself. I don't want to think about it,' said Andy.

'Hear! Hear!' said several men at once.

'No talking!' shouted a soldier.

They stood in a line against the far wall of the compound, in direct sunlight. It was already hot mid-morning. Some of the men were aware of how hot it would get. None of them had head covering and most wore only thin shirts.

The two soldiers stood facing them, with their weapons at the ready.

'I don't like this. I think they're going to keep us here in the sun,' mused Andy. 'We've no water and no protection. It won't be long before we begin to suffer.'

An hour later, Andy was proved right. The lack of very much air movement in the compound, the light-coloured walls and floor and the sun pouring down relentlessly, had become extremely uncomfortable for most, and unbearable for several of the men.

After two hours, most of them were on their knees, unable to remain standing.

'How much longer? This will kill us,' opined Philips.

'It will take more than this to kill us, Philips, but it will make us very weak, and cause us a great deal of discomfort. Bear up, old chap, we're still alive, and as they say, where there's life, there's hope,' said John, one of the doctors who didn't usually say a lot.

Philips was not in the mood to bear up, and he glared at John. 'Damn fool,' he muttered.

'No talking!' shouted a soldier.

After another hour, not one of the men was still standing. They were all hunched up on the ground. Nobody was talking. Their mouths were too dry to talk.

Two men, dressed in civilian Arab clothes came into the compound, pulling behind them a long hose.

They positioned themselves about twenty feet from the hostages and then the water was turned on.

Directing a powerful flow of water from side to side, they drenched the captives.

The water was not too cold. It was impossible for anything to be cold in this country. But it was very much colder than the men.

Some of them tried to catch some water in their hands to drink, but most turned their backs to it. It was too painful to bear on the front of their bodies. The shock of the water was too much for three of the men and they had collapsed, apparently unconscious. One of the doctors was kneeling over an unconscious body.

The water continued to pour until the ground was turned to mud. Those who tried to stand slipped and fell in the slippery mess.

A soldier shouted something in Arabic, and the water was turned off.

'Thank God!' said Steven. 'I'm surprised they had that much water in the whole of this country.'

'It must be a precious commodity for sure. They obviously have a well,' said Andy. 'Are you OK?'

'I will be, I think. I don't think I could have stood much more of either the sun or the water.'

'I think they know exactly what they're doing. This was a tried and tested torture.'

'Oh, you think so. Devious bastards,' said Steven forcefully.

Andy smiled and patted Steven gently on his back.

'Ouch!' said Steven.

'Sorry!' said Andy. They both laughed.

'No laughing! No Talking!' shouted the soldier. Andy and Steven laughed again.

'We'll be all right, you'll see,' said Andy.

# 21

The paras landed safely and established a stronghold in the rocks as suggested by the colonel. They radioed their position and readiness to HQ.

'Go, go, go!' shouted the colonel, to the mobile unit under the command of Lieutenant Willis.

'Right, Sergeant, take 'em away!'

'Yes, Sir! Waggons roll!'

'Enough of that, Sergeant, this is serious.'

'I know Sir, I'm sorry.'

The two large, heavily armoured vehicles lumbered off, accelerating quickly, flanked by the Oshkosh, behaving like a very large Jack Russell terrier.

The distance to the compound was less than twenty miles and the three vehicles made good time reaching the rendezvous with the paras who had reccied the target and devised a strategy for the attack. A total of thirty men prepared to storm the compound.

'I need four men to scale the wall and suss out the layout,' said Willis.

'Done that, Sir,' said Major Flack, in charge of the paras. 'The compound is approximately eighty feet across. At the far end is a blockhouse. A corridor takes you to the place where the hostages are being held. Beyond that is the barracks. We don't know how many men are there, Sir.'

'How did you find out all that?' asked Willis, incredulous.

'We're paras, Sir. Don't waste any time, Sir.'

'Well done, Major. Well, OK. Have you got a plan as well?'

'Of course, Sir.'

The major explained his plan to Willis and the two groups prepared to scale the compound walls. Any noise the attackers made would alert the enemy so speed was essential. A barrage of stun grenades was ready to quell any opposition.

Men climbed the walls in four places, grouping in the centre before attacking the building.

There was only one door into the building.

The first man through was shot by a burst of Kalashnikov fire.

The second man fell over the body and returned rifle fire from the prone position, but was himself severely injured. Already, the planned 'softly softly no lethal weapons' idea of Colonel Rogerson had quickly been abandoned.

'Stand back, take cover!' shouted Willis. 'Sergeant, grenades!'

The sergeant didn't need to be told, he, and two privates had positioned themselves either side of the doorway and lobbed in three anti-personal grenades. They had an effective killing range of more than forty feet and would clear the way for the rest of the men to enter the building.

The gunfire and explosions would have alerted any of the enemy in the barracks area. It would soon be clear what the attackers were up against.

Willis was worried. This wasn't how he had envisioned the attack. Two men down already.

Acting under the sergeant's orders, five men entered the building, rifles and grenade launchers at the ready No more shots were heard. The sergeant led a further four men in.

The paras, acting independently under the command of Major Flack had ignored Willis's approach and blown a hole in the roof of the building, through which they entered and disabled the guards. They soon found the cellar where the hostages were held and released them. Major Flack radioed to Willis, 'Cease fire! We have the hostages safely.'

Thinking they could have done without Willis's men, the Major triumphantly led the hostages out into the sun again.

That appeared to be that. The hostages were led to the two troop carrier vehicles and sent on their way with Sergeant Wilson driving the lead vehicle.

The rescued men were very quiet. There was no cheering or back slapping. They were exhausted, hungry and thirsty.

The remaining attack group, now assembled in the compound, were assessing the mission.

'Bit of a mess, wasn't it,' admitted Willis. Two men dead. All my fault of course. I shouldn't have sent them in.'

Major Flack was magnanimous. 'You did what you thought was right. Don't blame yourself. It could have been a lot worse. If there had been more ragheads or had they'd been better armed or better warned, who knows. As it is, we got the guys out, safe and sound.'

'You did, Sir, all on your own. I didn't contribute anything.'

'It was good to know you were there, Lieutenant, we needed to know we had back up if needed. Really, Willis, don't be hard on yourself. We did well, all of us.'

The men were relaxing. Most of them sitting or lying on the sandy floor of the compound. A small group was busy checking the dead Taliban soldiers in the building.

But all was not well. A Taliban cell not far away had heard the explosions and gunfire and was on its way to investigate.

Well-armed and motivated, the Taliban is a formidable adversary. He knows the country and he knows his enemy. Under the command of Abdul Ahmed Zahed, this group was well known to the British and American troops.

There was no warning. First, smoke grenades, then high explosive grenades came over the wall.

'Take cover!' several men shouted unnecessarily.

Grabbing their carelessly dropped weapons, the soldiers made for the cover of the building. Two men had fallen victim to the grenades and four men were trying to drag them to safety.

Before they had all taken cover in the building, the Taliban were swarming over the wall, firing their Kalashnikovs and filling the air with bullets. Two more soldiers fell.

Once inside, the soldiers had lost any advantage they might have had. The only way in or out was the small doorway which allowed only single file movement. One man and a machine gun might have been able to defend the building but there was no machine gun. Willis had stipulated softly softly and non-lethal weapons. Fortunately, the British soldier always carries his rifle, but the only machine guns were on the vehicles, on their way back to base.

The para major quickly assumed command and was giving orders. All the paras regained the roof through the hole they had blown, and were already laying down a barrage of fire into the compound.

The remaining soldiers took up positions in the various rooms in the building, ready to pick off any Taliban that ventured inside.

The building was a nightmare to defend and almost as difficult to attack, as they had found out.

The Taliban were well equipped. They hadn't left their machine gun at home. They set up a captured American M2 50 calibre heavy machine gun, aiming it at the doorway. This effectively trapped the men in the building. At least, it would have done. The whole unit scrambled through the hole and joined the paras. Now they had the advantage, adding their firepower to that of the paras they were soon able destroy the Taliban. The M2 had not fired a single 50 cal bullet.

'I suggest we head for home,' said Major Flack, thumping Willis's back enthusiastically.

'I'm with you on that,' said Willis.

# 22

Steven was telling his secretary about his holiday. He didn't want to alarm her with stories of abduction and torture.

'So, where was it you went? You didn't send me a postcard.'

I toured the Middle East, as many countries as I could. It's very hot and smelly in a lot of them, and the food is, well what shall I say, not like ours. I had a couple of bouts of Gippy tummy and Delli belly. They get the names from Egypt and Delhi you know, with good cause.'

'You've caught the sun, in fact you look a bit burned.'

'Yes, I fell asleep in the sun one day.'

After a few minutes answering Lydia's persistent questions Steven gave up. He couldn't lie to her any more.

'I'm sorry, Lydia, I lied to you. I haven't been on holiday. I was abducted by some terrorists. I didn't want to worry you, but as I'm back safe I suppose I can tell you.'

Lydia had to sit down. 'My God, Steven, how awful! Did they hurt you? Was it terrible?'

'Well, it was pretty bad, but they didn't actually hurt me. It was the conditions we were kept in that was the worst part.'

He went on to describe the whole episode, to the increasing concern of Lydia, who had put her arm around Steven's shoulder to comfort him. Steven enjoyed the closeness and realised just how much he felt for this attractive young woman.

It was a shock to realise that this new emotion was love, and he didn't know how to handle it.

He took Lydia's hand, and looking at her closely, and with dry mouth, managed to say, 'Lydia, I think I'm falling in love with you.'

'Oh, Steven. I love you! I have loved you for a long time, but couldn't tell how you felt about me.'

She hugged him and somehow they kissed. Steven had never kissed anyone before. It was a clumsy thing, but they were happy.

'I want to tell everyone,' said Lydia, beaming.

'Best not, I think, not in the office anyway, don't you think?' cautioned Steven, who also had a broad grin.

'Does this mean we're engaged,' asked Steven, naively.

'You have to ask me to marry you, then we would be engaged,' said Lydia hopefully.

'In that case, Lydia, my love, will you marry me?' said Steven, his confidence increasing exponentially.

'I will, I will, Oh Steven, I do love you!'

'Do you go to church?' he asked, realising how little he knew of Lydia.

'Yes, I do. I go to St Stephen Walbrook. It's near Bank station. It's one of Sir Christopher Wren's, built in 1679. Christopher Wren himself worshipped there. Oh, I'm sorry, I tend to go on a bit about my church. What about you? Oh, you aren't Catholic are you?'

Steven laughed. 'No, that would make it difficult wouldn't it? No, I'm Anglican, although not a regular churchgoer I'm afraid. When I do go, it's to St Michael's, Wood Green, just down the road from my flat. It's very modern, and to be honest, I didn't like it when I first went there, but it grows on you.'

'Sounds nice. We will have to go together, to both churches. We can decide which one to be married in.'

'Isn't it usual to get married in the bride's church?'

'Yes, but it's nor compulsory.'

'This is rather exciting. This morning I had no idea that by coffee time I would be engaged to be married!' Steven was smiling so much his sunburned face began to hurt. It wasn't used to this expression.

The rest of the day was a blur. Later, Steven couldn't remember what had happened. Apart from getting engaged of course.


In the following weeks, they visited both churches and decided on Steven's in which to marry. They tentatively fixed a date, arranged to meet the Rector of St Michael's and Lydia spent a long time looking at wedding dresses and clothes suitable for a honeymoon. But they hadn't decided where that would be. Except that Steven had said definitely not the Middle East.

But, like many plans that gang agley, things didn't work out smoothly.

Steven was contacted by Bernard. They had a job for him.

# 24

Steven drove to Chalgrove Airfield and reported for duty at the headquarters.

He had bought the car only a few days before being summoned and was glad of the chance to take a drive and get used to the car. He was not happy to be called for another assignment so soon.

He and Lydia had browsed around the car showrooms all day before plucking up courage to go into the Porche showroom in Berkely square.

They were welcomed enthusiastically by a smartly dressed salesman.

'Good afternoon, Sir, Madam. How can I help you?'

'We would just like to look at some cars, if that's all right,' said Steven.

'Well, you've come to the right place,' smirked the salesman. 'Did you have a particular model in mind?

'None at all, we'd like to see what you have.'

They looked at the rows of shining cars, rather bemused by the technical patter of their host. Steven thought they all looked very similar.

'I like this one,' said Lydia pointing to a 911.

'How much is this one?' Steven asked, innocently.

'That's the 911 fifty-year anniversary model, Sir. It is rather special, hence the price, two-hundred thousand pounds.'

Steven took a moment to take that in. 'Gosh,' he said at last.

'We do have less expensive cars, Sir. Something like a Boxster, perhaps, they start at fifty-eight thousand pounds?'

'Well, yes, I'm sure. I'm afraid these cars are a bit too pricey for us. I'm sorry to have troubled you.'

'Perhaps you would consider a used car, Sir. Our branch has a good selection.'

'Oh, let's look at some second-hand ones, Steven. I do like them,' urged Lydia, excitedly.

'Here is the address of our used car branch, Sir,' said the salesman, handing Steven a card.

They hurried from the showroom, somewhat shaken by the cost of a new Porche.

'I'm not sure we could afford even a second-hand one, Love,' said Steven, thinking that a second-hand Volkswagen Golf might be more suitable.

But Lydia was determined, and by the end of the day they were the proud owners of a Boxster, a few years old and with quite a lot of miles on its clock. Steven thought the price of eleven thousand pounds a bit steep for a second-hand car, but Lydia was happy, and the car was very nice. It had been well cared for and wore its miles well.

The M40 was an ideal road on which to test the Porche's capabilities.

He was enjoying this little car. It was very comfortable and beautifully equipped. The radio, playing Classic FM, filled the car with Brahms' Violin Concerto. Steven hummed along with the familiar themes.

After about fifty miles, Steven glanced at the speedometer and was alarmed to see that he was doing over a hundred miles per hour. The car wasn't even trying. 'Oh, dear,' he muttered. 'I shall have to be careful.'

By the time he left the M40 at Lewknor, to take the B4009, he felt confident in the Boxster, and admitted that Lydia's choice had been a good one.

'New car, old man?' said Bernard by way of a greeting, as the guard opened the gates to the private airfield.

'Yes, it is, as a matter of fact. Do you like it?'

'Indeed I do, perhaps you would allow me to take her for a little spin?'

'Of course,' said Steven, reluctantly, thinking that Bernard would have a job getting in the little car.

There were only four people at the meeting in the tiny unmarked office. Bernard, William, Steven and the agent Steven only knew as three-seven-oh.

'Now, this is just between the four of us, you understand? You must not under any circumstances talk, even to another agent, about it.' Began Bernard, without preamble. He had a stern expression and there were no jokey asides.

'This job requires two agents working closely together.'

'You've heard of Seran Dascovar no doubt. Yes?'

The two agents nodded, although Steven had never heard the name.

'Dascovar is head of a large gang of criminals working in Serbia and Bosnia Herzegovina. Unofficially known as the Serbian Mafia. Their activities cover the entire spectrum of crime, mainly in Belgrade. Up until now we have left it to the Srpske Policija, don't ask me the correct pronunciation, they are the national police and generally effective. But it has come to our notice that the said Dascovar has extended his activities to include arms dealing, and we don't like that. It's your job to stop him. You've got reservations at the Golden Tulip Hotel in the names in your false passports; Edmund Stansgate and Giusseppe Faro. They were real people, that's how we got the passports.

Dascovar likes to eat at The Petit Chef, a restaurant not far from your hotel. Understand?'

'When you say stop him . . .' ventured three seven oh.

'You don't mean kill him?' said Steven.

143

'How else do you think you'll stop him? Of course kill him! Idiots!'

'But isn't that a job for double 0s?'

'You watch too many James Bond films, my lad. All agents are licenced to kill. How on earth could we manage if only half a dozen agents could kill?'

'But we are only part-time agents,' protested Three-seven-oh.

'Agents just the same. Now, less complaints if you don't mind; we have work to do.'

Bernard handed packets of documents and information to each agent.

'Now, there's a hundred and fifty thousand dinars each. That should be enough. That's roughly a thousand pounds. I don't expect you to be there more than a week. And there's some emergency US dollars – the universal currency, but don't use them unless you have to, OK. There's a thousand bucks there,' he said, handing them both wads of notes. Put it somewhere safe.'

'But why two of us?' asked three-seven-oh. 'And why us?' We don't have the experience for this sort of thing.'

'So that neither one of you will accept responsibility for the death of the target of course. You have a lot to learn. And how are you going to learn if you don't do the job?'

'I see, I think,' mumbled three-seven-oh.

'Is that clear, four-four-two?'

'I guess so,' said Steven.

'Right, off you go. Your flight is from Heathrow at eight-thirty. Dobro putovanje!'

'I guess that means Bon voyage, or I should say Buon viaggio,' whispered three-seven-oh,.' as they left the office.

'Look, can't we use our real names if we're going to be working together?' suggested Steven as they got into the Alfa.

'Sure, I'm Mario. You're Steven, I believe?'

'That's right. Good to meet you, Mario. You're Italian?'

'Of course.'

'But you have no accent and you speak English perfectly.'

'Well, I should. I did my degree at Oxford and I've lived in Britain for twenty years.'

'What's your subject? What did you read?'

'PPE, boring as hell, but it's what a lot of top employers like. I did politics and international relations.'

'Useful in this game,' said Steven.

'Yes, of course, and I speak five European languages as well. Unfortunately, Serbian isn't one of them!' he laughed.

'I read English at Cambridge. Very enjoyable, but not a lot of use,' Steven said, 'and I only speak French, badly, and a little Welsh, worse!'

'Never mind, my friend, you can, no doubt recite poetry, it will be nice when we're up against insuperable odds.'

145

'Huh, yes, that's about all I can do. I don't know what I'm doing in this lark.' He was warming to this new companion. He seemed to have a better idea what he was doing.

Mario declined to comment; he selected a gear and accelerated away from the airfield. The little car was soon doing sixty miles an hour to the accompaniment of a rich exhaust note.

# 25

The two men were content to listen to the pleasant noises made by the car on the little roads leading to the motorway, but the exhaust note became monotonous when the car settled into a steady motorway speed.

'What is the plan, my friend?' asked Mario after about half an hour.

'There isn't one, as far as I know. Just kill this Dascovar character. Just like that!' he imitated a well-known comedy magician's trademark phrase, and tried to laugh.

Mario either didn't know the television personality or Steven's impersonation was so bad, he didn't make the connection.

'Just like a what? Howa we goin' to do 'im?' Mario replied in an artificial Italian accent that made Steven laugh.

'Seriously, my friend. Have you any ideas at all?'

'I haven't had time for it to sink in yet, never mind how we're going to do it.'

'How long have we got?'

'We're booked in to the hotel for two weeks and our return air tickets are dated two weeks from today as well. It doesn't give us much time.'

'What about weapons?'

'We can't take guns on the plane, so I don't know.'

'You are new to this, my friend, there are ways. I will show you,' said Mario, confidently. 'Do you fancy a break; we could stop at a service station,' he added, slowing the car.

'There's nothing until Beaconsfield Services, that's not bad. I could do with something,' said Steven.

'OK, put it in the sat-nav, see how far it is.'

'It'll be about forty miles I reckon, not far.'

'You've been there before, huh?'

'Couple of times, yes. It's quite good. They have a good choice of food.'

By the time they had parked and browsed a dozen different places to eat, they decided on *el Mexicana,* although that was not really Steven's choice. He was more of a fish and chips man. He did enjoy the burrito, but found it a bit messy to eat.

It was getting dark by the time they had eaten, and drunk two cups of coffee each.

'I will take you home, Steve, we meet again tomorrow early, and get to the airport in plenty of time. We can discuss our plans on the way. OK?'

'OK by me, yes. I'm so tired now, I can't think at all.'

When Mario dropped him at his flat, he was looking forward to getting a good night's sleep. He was worried about this new job, and he wasn't happy about having to work with Mario, who, although obviously experienced, was also a little too flippant and cocksure. He was easy to talk to, and in other circumstances Steven felt he would make a good friend. But over confidence was dangerous in this sort of work. But, like it or not, he was stuck with this man. He would just have to be extra careful.

For the third or fourth time he checked his passport and visa, and his money. He flipped through the wad of Serbian dinar notes. He was fascinated by banknotes and had been particularly sorry to see the beautiful French notes replaced by the boring Euros which he thought looked like monopoly money. These ex-USSR countries at least, had a little imagination. Some of the Serbian notes had pictures of Nikolas Tesla, one of the country's heroes.

Despite being tired, he could not sleep. Too many frightening images kaleidoscoped around in his mind. In the end he got up and looked at his emails. After a while he did doze, but the images would not go away, and when Mario sounded the horn of the Alfa to signify his arrival, he had been dreaming he and Mario were about to be shot by a firing squad.

'Ok, I'm coming, give me a minute!' he shouted from the window.

'Plenty of time, don't rush!' called Mario.

The drive to the airport was not spent discussing plans. Neither man had any idea how they were going to carry out this delicate operation. Nor did any ideas materialise on the flight.

As soon as they saw Belgrade's ultra-modern Nikola Tesla Airport Steven realised he would have to seriously modify his preconceptions of Serbia. He had imagined drab, communist style buildings and shabbily dressed peasants struggling to eke a living from a colourless land. Instead, he was amazed to find beautiful buildings with well-dressed and cheerful people in a beautiful country with breathtaking landscapes and a fascinating history.

The two men booked into the splendid Golden Tulip Zera Hotel, astonished at the very reasonable cost of a room, and agreed to meet in the lobby later.

'Is this a country troubled by organised crime?' Steven mused.

The room was plainly furnished, but everything was of good quality and scrupulously clean. Steven lay on the bed and closed his eyes.

'Come on, my friend, what are you doing?' Mario shouted while banging on Steven's door.

Steven had fallen asleep. He let Mario in.

'OK, OK, I know, I'm tired, too. And worried. We have to do this. How are we going to find this guy?' said Mario, sitting on the bed while Steven tidied himself.

'Yes, I know. The best places to look for Seran Dascovar are posh gambling joints, casinos and the like. According to William anyway. So, I suggest we make a list and visit some; get an idea of the lie of the land. What do you say?'

'Well yes, of course. I'll ask reception to give us some information.'

'Oh, I meant to ask you before – did you manage to get weapons?'

Mario laughed, patting his jacket pocket. 'Of course! You like the Smith and Wesson CSX 9mm I understand, there you are. No holster I'm afraid. It has the ten-round mag, fully loaded, but there's no spare ammo. I like the Sig Sauer P320 compact myself,' he patted his pocket again, and smiled.

'How did you get them through?'

'I told you, there are ways. But I keep to myself.'

'You're a genius!' said Steven, caressing the Smith and Wesson.

'Yes, I am!' laughed Mario. 'And now we are ready to dispatch this objectionable little man.'

'Do we even know what he looks like.'

'We'll soon find out, when we start asking around.'

'That could be dangerous,' cautioned Steven.

'Of course, but we will flush him out, huh?'

# 26

Steven was not happy about Mario's careless attitude but there was nothing he could do about it.

The next three days, or rather evenings and nights, were spent in the city's gambling establishments. Keeping their ears open for any mention of their quarry. They gambled, modestly, and won a little, and lost a little. They mixed with the customers and bought drinks for the young women who decorated the bars. Nobody mentioned Dascovar, or any suggestion of crime of any kind. It all seemed remarkably civilised.

One evening, Mario was getting very friendly with one of the young women and suggested they find somewhere less crowded.

'Oh, no, I can't. Seran would not like that.'

'Who is Seran, your boyfriend?' asked Mario, innocently.

'He is the boss. He likes us girls to stay at the bar to entertain the customers.'

'Do you mean you're employed to do this,'

Of course, I would have thought you realised that,' said the girl.

Mario was somewhat deflated, he had thought he was making a conquest. 'So, who is this Seran? Is he about? I would like to meet him.'

'He moves about among his clubs. He could be anywhere. But really, Sir – I would not recommend you met him.' She lowered her eyes.

'Why ever not, one businessman to another, surely . . .'

'No, please, you must not. I have to go!'

She slid off the bar-stool and ran, awkwardly on absurdly high heeled shoes, and disappeared through a door at the end of the bar.

Steven had been watching this exchange and moved casually over to the bar.

He ordered a scotch and water and moved slowly towards Mario. They had agreed not to appear to be together.

'What was all that about?' he whispered.

'Tell you in a minute,' he said quietly, then, loud enough for anyone nearby to hear, 'I'm going outside for a smoke.'  As he passed Steven, he whispered, 'Join me after a few minutes.'

There was a terrace alongside the bar which was frequented by smokers. A minute or two later Steven wandered out and lit a cigarette. He was not a smoker but often bought a pack of cigarettes as they could be a good icebreaker and he had learned to pretend convincingly.

There was no sign of Mario.

Without appearing to have anything to worry about, Steven slowly paced up and down the terrace, looking in alcoves and through windows for any sign of his colleague.

His cigarette finished, Steven drifted back into the bar, scanning the room for a sight of Mario.

Ten minutes later and still no sign, Steve was seriously worried. He didn't know what to do.

He had some gambling chips in his pocket. He decided to cash them in and return to his hotel. Mario would know where to find him.

'Going so soon, Sir?' said the cashier, handing over a few hundred dinars.

'Yes, I have a headache,' Steven improvised. 'Good night!'

Steven took a taxi back to the Golden Tulip. He debated with himself whether to sit in the lounge or go to his room. He decided he might attract attention if he were to stay long in the lounge so went to his room. He hadn't been aware of anyone watching him.

But someone evidently had been, because there was a note pushed under the door.

Steven picked it up nervously.

*Leave Belgrade immediately. For your own safety.* The note was handwritten and its message was clear. They, whoever they were, were on to them. They had probably given Mario the same message.

But they had a job to do. Mario would feel the same, surely. They had an obligation. It was not something from which they could just opt out.

For the umpteenth time, Steven checked his gun, taking out the magazine and counting the cartridges. He pulled back the slide and pulled the trigger. All working perfectly. He replaced the magazine and put the gun back in his pocket. It wasn't very heavy but it did pull his jacket out of shape a little. He wished he had his custom-made holster.

He took the gun out once more, it felt good in his hand. He was a competent shot, but could he kill a man? He had secretly hoped that Mario would do the deed. He had seemed not to be worried at the prospect. But he was not here. If he didn't turn up it would be up to Steven on his own.

'Oh Dear!' he said. 'Another fine mess you've got yourself into.' He managed a little smile at the recollection of Oliver Hardy's famous expression.

After a little while he decided it would be safe to wait in the hotel lounge and hope Mario would return. There was a magazine rack with current newspapers from all the European countries. Steven selected a copy of The Times and settled down to read it, while keeping one eye on the door.

Mario, meanwhile, was being entertained by a group of nasty looking henchmen of the arch criminal Seran Dascovar, the reason for their being in Serbia, His hands were tied behind his back and he sat on a stool.

'What you do in Belgrade?' asked the biggest of the men, for the fifth time.

'I told you; I am on holiday and I like a little gamble.'

You don't have to come all the way to Serbia to gamble. Why are you here?'

'Let me have a go at him,' said a little bearded man, brandishing a large knife.

'No, we must not hurt him. Well not too much anyway,' said the big man, who seemed to be in charge. 'We will rough him up a bit, but there must be no blood. Just bruises, you understand?'

This was all for Mario to hear, clearly. But Mario had been well trained. He was not unduly bothered.

He didn't react at all when the big man suddenly hit him, hard, in the abdomen. A blow that would have crippled a lesser man.

'Oh, so we have a professional!' he exclaimed. 'He is trained to take pain. We'll see how much he can take.'

'Let me do him, 'pleaded the little man.

'Later. He's mine now,' insisted the torturer.

He hit Mario again, in the same place. Mario could not help making a noise.

'Ahah, not so tough. Try this!' He hit Mario low down on his back, where he judged his kidneys were.

Mario groaned.

Again, and again. Mario was sweating. He gritted his teeth.

'Why are you here?' asked the man, quietly.

'Why are you here?' he shouted in Mario's ear.

'Holiday,' mumbled Mario.

The next blow was to Mario's knee, with a baseball bat.

Mario cried out.

'Got you!' said the man, gleefully. 'Why are you here?'

'Go to hell!' grunted Mario.

The other knee. Crack!

'You bastard!' shouted Mario.

'OK, you can have him now,' the big man said, wiping his hands on a dirty handkerchief. 'No blood, OK?'

'Sure, not where it will show anyway.'

'If you bleed him Seran will bleed you. You just hit him, understand?'

'Yes, I get it.'

The little man, eagerly watched by the others in the group, took up his position in front of the seated Mario. He kicked his victim's feet and legs apart, exposing his most vulnerable areas.

Mario braced himself. His scream delighted the men. They watched eagerly as the little man lined up the baseball bat again and landed another vicious blow to Mario's groin. He didn't cry out this time, he passed out.

'You idiot, you hit him too hard! Give me the bat.' The big man took the bat and hit the little man on the head with it, knocking him down.

'Can't trust anyone to do a simple job,' he grumbled. 'Leave them both for now. We come back later.'

Mario, who had feigned unconsciousness until the men had left, began struggling against his bonds.

He had been badly hurt, but not as badly as his captors thought. He was tough - he'd trained for this sort of situation. Soon, he was able to get his hands free, then it was a simple matter to untie the rope around his body.

The little man who had wanted so much to hurt Mario, still lay unconscious on the floor. Mario left him there when he cautiously opened the door. They had not thought it necessary to post a guard, the corridor was clear.

It was quite dark in the corridor and Mario was able to move almost invisibly in and out of the many alcoves and doorways. He had no idea where he was going or where his captors were.

Hearing voices coming from somewhere ahead, he moved even more carefully, stopping in doorways longer each time and checking the coast was clear before moving on.

He could identify the voice of the big man who was shouting angrily. He peered through a gap in window blind and could see a group of about a dozen men dressed similarly – not exactly uniform, but close.

Mario quickly moved away. He could see lights at the end of the corridor. The way out.

The lights were in a small square with drab buildings on three sides. There was no indication what might be in them. The fourth side was taken up by a church and its door was open. Mario stood at the door, listening. All quiet. He went inside.

The elaborate interior, lit by hundreds of candles, suggested to Mario that it was an orthodox church, probably Greek. A Roman Catholic himself, he felt fairly comfortable in this sort of environment.

He hoped the priest would be cooperative. He had to take the chance. A shadowy figure emerged from the gloom.

'Sine moj, da li si povređen,' said the priest, coming closer.

'Father, I'm sorry. Do you speak English?'

'Of course, are you hurt?'

'Yes, I am, Father, and I need your help.'

'Of course,' said the priest again, 'if I can. Come, sit down.' He led Mario into the vestry.

'I need to get to the Golden Tulip Hotel. My colleague is there. '

'It is not very far from here; I can get someone to take you. I would myself but I have to take a service shortly,' said the cleric, looking anxiously at Mario's bruised face.

'Thank you, Father, God Bless you.'

'Bog te blagoslovio, sine mo. God Bless you, my son.'

A young man came and led Mario to his car. He spoke no English, but smiled encouragingly. Mario's injuries were hurting a lot and he just smiled back.

When Mario saw Steven in the hotel lobby he almost cried.

'My God, Mario!' Steven exclaimed. 'What happened?'

'Just get me to my room and I'll explain,' mumbled Mario, grateful for the support of Steven's arm.

Room service had provided soup and coffee. Mario was feeling a little better.

'At least now we know what we're up against,' said Mario, after Steven had tended his injuries.

'I think this Dascovar guy has a small army doing his dirty work, and they are very nasty people.'

'What are we going to do?' asked Steven.

'Kill the bastard, of course!' exclaimed Mario passionately.

'Well yes, I know that, but how?'

'I'm working on it,' said Mario, with a wry smile.

# 27

It had been a while since Mario's return to the hotel and he was still in a great deal of pain. Steven had decided to let him rest.

Steven's mobile phone rang. He had forgotten to set it to silent. It was Lydia.

'Hello, love, what's the matter? You know you're not supposed to phone me when I'm working.'

'I'm sorry, I was worried. I haven't heard from you and you said it would be a few days.'

'I said I thought it might only be a few days. I can't predict how things will work out.'

'Are you all right, though.'

'Yes, yes, I'm OK. Now please don't phone again. I hope to see you soon.'

Ever since confiding in Lydia, he had regretted it. It was strictly forbidden to tell anyone what agents were doing and who they are, and for a very good reason. He didn't know what the penalty was for breaking the official secrets act but he was sure it would be severe.

He loved Lydia but he was often irritated by her. He wondered if there was a future in their relationship. If he broke it off, she would probably tell people about his being an agent. That would not do. 'Oh Dear!' he sighed loudly. 'What a mess.'

He then realised he had been thinking aloud and wondered if the room was bugged. 'Why would it be bugged?' again he verbalised his thoughts. 'Oh Dear!' he said again. 'I'm a fool'.

But, why would he think the room might be bugged? Mario's experience proved that someone did indeed know that they were in Belgrade. But they could not know what they were there for. Perhaps they bug the rooms of all foreigners. It is not so long since this was a part of the Soviet Union when everyone was under suspicion.

He was now convinced the room was bugged and began searching for anything that could conceal a tiny electronic device. He upturned table lamps, looked behind pictures and under ashtrays, opened drawers and cupboards, examined all the bottles in the mini-bar and even looked at the bar of soap in the bathroom, still wrapped in cellophane. He couldn't find a bug; but that didn't mean there wasn't one, he told himself. He was sweating.

'What did you say?' called Mario, weakly from his bed.

'Nothing, sorry. Go to sleep.'

'Who called?'

'Nobody.'

'I heard the phone, who was it?'

'Lydia.'

'That woman is a menace, Steve, you'll have to get rid of her.'

'I couldn't do that!'

'I don't mean kill her, you idiot. Just dump her.'

'She would talk if I did.'

'Who would believe her?'

'No, I suppose not, but it would be risky.'

'Not as risky as if you keep her on and she lets the cat out of the bag while we're on a job.'

'God, no! You're right. Oh Dear!'

'Think about it.'

'Do you think they bug the rooms?'

'What?'

'Do they bug the rooms?'

'Why would they?'

'Because we're foreigners.'

'Because I'm Italian you mean?'

'No, we're both foreigners here. They got used to being suspicious of foreigners under communism.'

'I think they're still communists, aren't they?'

'Maybe, but not soviets.'

'You'll give yourself a breakdown. Have a drink or something.'

'I'm sorry. How are you feeling? Do you want a drink?'

'I'll be all right. Just sore, more or less all over, that's all. I'll mend.' Mario laughed. Ýes I'll have a drink. What's in the bar?'

Steve called from the bar, 'There's a bottle of wine, tamjanika, never heard of that, some elderflower syrup and vinjak, from what I can gather from the label it's a sort of brandy, and there's rakija, that's brandy, too, I think. Probably made from plums. Oh, and I saw another smaller bottle of rakija in the frig. From what it says on the label I think that might be made from quinces. I find their language very difficult. What do you fancy?'

'Is there any coke?'

'Oh yes, I didn't think you'd want a soft drink.'

'I'll have a - vinjak, is it? And coke.'

'OK, coming up.'

Mario took a generous sip, and coughed. 'More coke in it please!'

'What's it like?' asked Steve, pouring more coke into Mario's glass.

'It's good!' croaked Mario, laughing and choking at the same time. Try it. It's a bit like sucking petrol from a tank, but, yeah, good!'

Steve poured himself a glass, with less vinjak and a lot more coke. They both laughed. They needed to relieve the tension of the last few days.

After a few more vinjak and cokes both men were feeling a lot better. Mario's injuries didn't hurt as much and Steven had stopped worrying about bugs.

'What do we do now?' asked Steven. 'Are we any nearer to finding Dascovar?'

'We know he has a lot of very nasty people working for him and I reckon he's in the city somewhere. He won't show himself. These big-time crooks keep themselves well hidden. The authorities can't pin anything on him. I'm known now, so you'll have to have a try. I can give you descriptions of the guys that beat me up. They are the link, I'm sure.'

Steven reluctantly agreed. He had to do his bit. He didn't fancy a beating but poor Mario had suffered enough.

The next evening, Steven went to the club where Mario had met Dascovar's cronies.

All the gaming tables were well occupied but he saw a space at the roulette table and squeezed in. Nodding to the people either side.

'*Faites vos jeux, messieurs, dames*,' called the croupier. Steven quickly put a brightly coloured chip on the nearest square before the croupier called, '*Rien ne va plus!*'

'Your lucky night, monsieur!' whispered the young woman next to him, 'You've won!'

'What? Have I? I don't know how to play. How did you know I was English?'

I heard you at the cashier desk. Now, what are you going bet on this time?'

Steven chose a chip and placed it on a square next to his winning one. 'There, try that,' he said, and the girl put her chip on the same square.'

'*Rien ne va plus!*' called the croupier as the wheel spun, sending the little ball dancing round the rim.

'You've won again!' exclaimed the girl. The croupier frowned at her. 'Sorry!' she said.

Beginners luck stayed with Steven with almost every other spin of the wheel and after an hour or so at the table his wins were much greater than his losses and he had a substantial pile of brightly coloured chips. He decided to stop.

He wanted a drink. The croupier nodded as he left the table. The girl clung to his arm. He didn't object. She was very attractive. She said her name was Mila.

'Do you want a drink?' Steven asked after cashing in his winnings and stuffing the thick wad of notes into his inside jacket pocket. He tried to estimate how much he had won. He couldn't remember the exchange rate but he knew a million dinars was not really a fortune. Maybe not a great deal then, but nice, he thought.

'Yes, please. Can we have champagne?' Mila purred.

It was getting late. Steven didn't know what to do with the girl. She had drunk too many glasses of champagne and was hanging on to his arm.

A smartly dressed young man appeared at the door, scanning the gaming room.

He was coming straight towards Steven.

'There you are, Mila! Ko je to?

'He's English,' whispered Mila.

'What you do with my girl?' The man spoke heavily accented English.

'What? I just played roulette with her, that's all,' he said, weakly.

'Andrej! Dođi ovde,' he shouted.

The bartender, tall dark and mean-looking, came over, 'Šta je to, Seran?'

Dascovar gestured him to be quiet.

'What you do here, English, with my girl?

'I was just playing roulette and she sat next to me. I won and we had a drink.'

'Nobody messes with Seran Dascovar's girl!' the man growled, looking Steven in the eye. Steven could smell alcohol on his breath. This is Dascovar, he thought. I've got to kill this man, if I don't, he's going to kill me.

Dascovar nodded to the bartender, and before Steven had a chance to resist, the two of them had his arms behind his back and were marching him towards a door marked Privatni.

Once inside, Steven was roughly searched and tied to a chair. Dascovar was delighted with Steven's pistol. He paid scant attention to the money. This man's thing was power, and it oozed from him. He waved the gun about, pretend shooting at pictures on the walls. He was laughing. Andrej was laughing, too, until the big man shut him up.

'Another fine mess . . .' thought Steven.

# 28

Steven had feared for his life when he was tied to the chair and Dascovar waved his gun menacingly. But the man was very drunk, and probably wouldn't have been able to shoot anyone if he'd wanted to but he would be able to carry out a beating like Mario's.

Andrej took Dascovar's arm and carefully prised the gun from his fingers.

'Come on now, chief, he'll keep. I'll get you some coffee.'

'I don't want coffee! I want a drink! You hear me, a drink!' He pulled against Andrej and when the big man let go, he staggered and fell. Andrej tried to help him and in so doing dropped the gun.

He continued to support Dascovar, not seeming to notice the gun, which had fallen near Steven's feet.

While the two men were distracted Steven managed to get a foot to the gun and drag it under the chair. His two adversaries ignored him. He couldn't see what they were doing behind him. He kept still and quiet.

Gradually, sounds from the gaming room diminished until, after maybe an hour, everything was completely silent.

He set about trying to get out of his bonds.

Either Andrej had not been a Boy Scout or it really was Steven's lucky day. By wriggling and pulling he got his arms loose. It was easy then to get his feet free.

The tables had turned. But what to do to take advantage. He checked the pistol's magazine. Still full.

He had no way of knowing how many of Dascovar's men were in the building.

The gun Mario had provided had the ten-round magazine, the same as the one he had back home, chosen because it was slightly smaller and lighter than the twelve-round magazine. He wished he had twelve rounds now. Something to remember if he ever got out of this.

He opened the door to the gaming room, through which the two men had exited. All was in darkness except for a dim light behind the bar.

Two men, looking startled, were coming towards Steven.

'Don't hesitate!' William had advised. He didn't. Choosing body shots as the bigger target, although he couldn't possibly miss at this range, he shot both men in quick succession. They fell noiselessly and he put another round in each of them to be sure. The sound of four gunshots would be sure to attract attention, so he quickly looked for the way out.

There was no reaction to the gunfire. The building seemed empty.

Stopping only to retrieve the thick wad of money from Dascovar's pocket, he'd won it after all, he left the building and walked quickly away, not looking back. There was nobody about.

Once satisfied he was clear and that nobody had seen him or followed him, Steven stopped to take stock, and sat in a shop doorway.

'Oh, my God!' he whispered harshly, breathing deeply. 'I shot two men!' He suddenly felt sick. He retched, but he hadn't eaten for such a long time his stomach was empty. He felt wretched. This was what he had feared most from being mixed up with the secret services. They had warned him. They'd given him a gun for goodness' sake. But he had hoped it would never happen. The fact that his victims had been killers themselves didn't help.

'Jeste li dobro, gospodine?' said a friendly voice.

'What?' he said, and looked up at a young woman in a dark blue uniform looking at him with a very concerned look on her face. He assumed she was a police officer.

'Oh, hello, Officer. I'm OK, bit too much to drink, I'm afraid.'

'Oh, you are English. Better come with me I think, you're not fit to be out on the street. Not a very nice neighbourhood this. What are you doing here anyway?' The policewoman had a grip on Steven's arm and didn't look like letting go.

Steven thought it best to say nothing, just carry on with the pretence of being under the influence.

It was not far to the police station. Steven was booked in as drunk and put in a cell.

'You aren't under arrest, sir, but you will be safe here until you sober up a bit,' the sergeant had said.

Although he wasn't drunk it suited him to pretend. The cell was reasonably comfortable. He slept.

He dozed and daydreamed of Afghanistan again, and of ducks, and about killing, and about Lydia. He felt worse.

He did sleep eventually, and so deeply he didn't dream. When a policeman gently shook his arm and showed him the big mug of coffee he'd brought, Steven managed a smile. He felt a little better. He remembered the events of the previous night vividly; he sat up and smiled again. 'I got the bastard!' he breathed.

'What was that, sir?' said the policewoman.

'Oh, you still here? Nothing. Something I dreamt, that's all.'

'Popijte čaj, gospodine. Biće parče tosta kad budeš spreman,' said the young policewoman, then quickly reverted to English, which she spoke perfectly, 'Drink your coffee, sir. There'll be a slice of toast when you're ready.'

Steven ate his toast and drank his coffee and was cautioned about drinking too much before

171

being sent on his way. He could not believe his gun had not been discovered. He hurried away from the police station and headed for the nearest taxi rank, to which the policemen had given him directions.

The taxi was a Škoda Fabia and its driver was a cheerful man keen to show his fare the city sights.

'No, please, just take me to the Golden Tulip Hotel,' said Steven, afraid he was in for an expensive trip.

'OK sir. Another time. Not expensive.'

In fact, the short ride to the hotel cost only five hundred Dinars, much to Steven's surprise. Less than a fiver he guessed. If travelling by taxi was so cheap, it was a wonder anyone owned a car in this city, he thought.

He hurried up to the room, looking forward to telling Mario what had happened.

Steven stood at the door, shocked to see, not Mario but Lydia, sitting at the desk.

'What on earth are you doing here? And where is Mario?' Steven blurted.

'That's a fine welcome, I must say!' said Lydia, sharply. 'I came to see how you were, as you don't phone. Mario has gone for cigarettes.'

'But how did you know we were here?'

'I went to your flat and found some information about Belgrade. I guessed that's where you were, and I was told the Golden Tulip was a favourite hotel for visitors. I took a chance. But it seems I was wasting my time. You aren't pleased to see me.' She turned away, sitting stiffly.

'It was a shock seeing you. Of course I'm pleased to see you, but you shouldn't have come. I've told you. It's dangerous. Very dangerous.'

Just then, Mario returned, and he too stood at the door. 'Steve, old man, you're back! How did you get on? Are you pleased to see Lydia?' he said, in a rush.

'Hello, Mario, yes, I'm back, miraculously. I am pleased and alarmed to see Lydia here. This is no place for a young woman. It's too dangerous. I have probably got the whole Serbian Mafia after me.'

'Tell me more. Did you find Dascovar?'

'I did, I can't tell you now, but the job is done.'

'What? You've killed him?'

'Shut up, you idiot.'

'Killed, did you say?' asked Lydia, anxiously.

'No, of course not. Figure of speech,' Steven improvised.

'I demand to know what's going on,' said Lydia, glaring at the two men.

'You're in no position to demand anything. I want you to go home, and stay there until I finish here. Say nothing to anyone. Do you hear? Nobody must know we are here. It's very important.' He had spoken sharply, but it was necessary. Lydia looked at him wide eyed and with her mouth open. She could hardly believe this was mild mannered Steven talking. After a minute or two, she calmed down. 'I'm sorry, I didn't think. I was worried about you. I'll go. Perhaps I will see you at home?'

'Of course. Come here.' Steve took her in his arms and gave her a reassuring hug and an awkward kiss.

'Off you go, now, there's a good girl. You haven't seen us, OK?'

After Lydia had gone, Steven told Mario the whole story.

'Well done, old man! Mission accomplished!'

'Just begun, I think. Dascovar was head of the Serbian Mafia, but from what I heard while I was with them, there are plenty more ready to take up cudgels.'

'But you don't understand the lingo.'

'I didn't need to understand, it was obvious. They were afraid of him. No, terrified is nearer. He was like a God almost. They will want to avenge his death I'm sure, but there are ones who would be pleased to take his place. And they aren't going to stop their plans for more terrorist action because Dascovar is dead either. We have to stop them.'

'That's fightin' talk, hombre,' said Mario, trying to lighten the situation.

'Listen. We've been given a job to find out who is responsible for the terrorist activity in the UK. Well, I think perhaps we've found part of them. But we can't just report back saying we've found them. They have to be dealt with. Somehow.

# 29

Steven sat quietly, thinking. Mario was smoking and complaining about the quality of the cigarettes he had just bought from the hotel bar.

'I wish I'd thought to bring a supply of decent cigarettes. How can anyone smoke these on a regular basis. I thought Italian cigarettes were pretty awful, but these!' He coughed for emphasis.

'Well don't smoke them, then,' advised Steven.

'I can't not smoke them, they are the only ones I have!' responded Mario, irritably. He coughed again to make his point.

'I mean don't smoke. They'll kill you.'

'You don't understand.'

'No, I don't. Just shut up about your cigarettes. What are we going to do about these terrorists?'

'I can't think without a decent cigarette. I don't know. What do you think?'

'You'd better have these if they're going to help you think,' said Steven, handing over the cigarettes he'd brought with him.

'You're a lifesaver! Where did you get English cigarettes? You don't smoke.'

'I often carry a packet. They come in handy sometimes.'

Mario lit up and sighed contentedly. 'That's better, good ones too!'

'I think it's too much for us. I reckon we are probably outnumbered by at least a hundred to one, just in Belgrade.

'Yes, but we're cleverer than them.'

'I wouldn't bank on that. They're pretty smart when it comes to fighting. And not only that, they're fanatics, they seem to regard lives cheaply. I don't think we have any chance of defeating them.'

'So, what do you think we should do?'

'You and me, I don't know. But looking at the bigger picture I think the only way the terrorism will end is for us, that is, all the western nations, to leave, completely – leave them to it. It's their country after all, and their religion. We don't like it, but we can't do anything about it.'

Mario's mouth had dropped open, he hadn't heard Steven talk like this before, in fact he hadn't heard Steven say much at all.

'You're mixing up the Taliban and the Serbian Mafia. Our job was to take out Dascovar. We've done that – or rather you've done that. So, what does the Serbian Mafia have to do with the Taliban?'

'You weren't involved in the Sword of Allah case were you. I'm sorry. Yes, I suppose I do tend to lump them together. They're all terrorists, and it's a common problem. So, we just give up, is that what you're saying?'

'But the Sword of Allah and the Taliban are clearly Islamic. Serbia is more than ninety percent Orthodox Christian, there are hardly any Muslims here. You can't say it's the same problem.'

In a way it is. They've said, very clearly, that they will not stop until we leave. From what I've seen, they mean what they say.'

'We're talking about two very different organisations,' insisted Mario. 'The Serbs haven't told us to leave. They don't actually know who we are.'

'But they have! didn't you get a note through your door? Of course they know who we are. And I'm sure Dascovar himself would have told us to leave if hadn't shot the – ' he struggled to find a suitable word. 'No, it isn't the same cause, but as far as we are concerned it might as well be. The results are the same. Terrorism is something we have to deal with. It doesn't matter which group of fanatics is responsible. And, to get back to my question – what are we going to do about it?' said Steven.

'I think we should go home and tell them we've done what we were sent here to do,' Mario spoke confidently.

'We've just made a start, that's all.'

'We have. Phone the airport; let's get out of here!' Mario was insistent.

Steven was glad the conversation was finished. He had been getting confused. He was tired. He could not wait to get home.

They were fortunate in getting seats on a Lufthansa Airbus A321 to Heathrow the next day. Both men were quietly excited at the prospect of being back in the UK.

They said very little on the flight. Mario drank too much whisky and slept, leaving Steven looking out of the window at eiderdowns of cloud that made him think – he could not have said why – of Lydia, who would be waiting impatiently to see him. But first he would have to report to HQ, and hope they would give him some time to recover.

Not for the first time since he had shot Dascovar, his thoughts sprang back; he remembered every detail, even how the trigger felt as he fired the fatal shots. He could see the surprised look on the faces of Dascovar and his henchman. He felt cold. He was a murderer. Nothing would ever take that away. It would be with him in every waking moment. He tried to convince himself that he was acting under orders and the deaths had been executions, justified maybe, but it didn't work.

He slept a little and dreamed dark dreams. He was glad when he woke, hearing the announcement that they were nearing their destination.

Reunited with his beloved Alfa, Mario cheered up, but didn't say much on the way to Chalgrove.

'I wish we didn't have to come all out here every time,' grumbled Steven.

'It's a pain, I agree, muttered Mario, as he braked hard at the gates to the airfield.

Bernard and William congratulated Steven and Mario for their successful mission. The two men handed back what was left of the money they had been given, but Steven said nothing about the stack of dinars he had won on the roulette table.

He was looking forward to seeing Lydia, he wanted to treat her, to make up for the harsh way he'd sent her packing.

But Lydia was not at home. It was Saturday, she wouldn't be at work. She wasn't expecting him. He hadn't told her he was coming home. There was no reason she should be at home. Even so, Steven felt uneasy. Something was not right. He decided to ask the neighbours if they'd seen her.

'No, I haven't seen her. She said she was going abroad for a few days last time I saw her,' said a middle-aged lady Steven met on the path near Lydia's little house.

'She usually drops in once or twice a week for a few bits of shopping, but I haven't seen her this week at all,' said the Indian shopkeeper in the corner shop at the top of Lydia's street.

Steven was reluctant to ask at the office because he didn't want to be interrogated by his boss about his absences. But he had to know if Lydia had been at work.

There was always a skeleton staff in the office in case of emergencies. They were not people Steven knew.

'Do you know Lydia Fowler? She's my secretary in procurement,' Steven asked the first person he saw when he entered the offices.

'Lydia, yes of course, I know her well. You won't find her here today, you should know that, she doesn't work weekends. And in any case she's on holiday. Gone somewhere, now what was it she said, Belgravia I think it was.' The young woman smiled.

Steven felt a chill down his back, and he suddenly felt a little lightheaded.

'Are you all right?' asked the young woman. 'I think you'd better sit down. I'll get you a drink. My name's Monica by the way. What's yours?'

'What? Oh, thank you. Steven. My name's Steven.'

Monica went off to get a drink, asking her colleague Elsie to keep an eye on the gentleman.

It didn't take Monica long to get a cup of coffee from the vending machine and she returned looking anxiously at Steven.

'Here you are, love. Drink this. You don't look too good, if you don't mind me saying. How do you feel?'

'Do you know this gentleman?' asked Elsie.

'He works in procurement. Lydia Fowler is his secretary.'

'Oh, I know her, she comes along here for coffee sometimes.'

'That's right, but I think she makes proper coffee for her boss.'

Steven was aware of the two women taking about him but he could only think about Lydia, who had taken time off to see him in Serbia and was now missing. He had sent her off rather abruptly, telling her to fly back home. Had she stayed in Belgrade? Hoping perhaps to see him again. He could not think. His mind was in turmoil.

The two women were still chattering. What do they do in the office on a Saturday, he wondered briefly.

He suddenly stood up, thanking the women for their concern and assuring them he was OK. He made for his own office along the corridor. He sat at his desk and picked up the telephone. There was no direct line, calls had to be made through the operator. Was she on duty at weekends? Evidently not. The phone was dead. 'Damn!' shouted Steven, smashing the handset down. He ran back down the corridor.

The two women were still in conversation.

'Where can I phone? The exchange is closed.'

'There's the emergency phone. That's always got a signal. It's independent of the usual system in case of well, emergencies of course,' she giggled.

'Yes, yes, but where is it?'

'It's in a glass case, you have to break the glass. Otherwise everybody would use it.'

'Yes, I understand, but where is it?' Steven was frantic.

'Just there on the wall,' said Elsie, pointing.

'Thank you,' said Steven, trying very hard to keep calm. He used his elbow to break the glass and took the mobile phone from its charging cradle. He looked at it and realised he didn't know who to phone.

'Think man!' he said. 'Who will know?'

The airline of course. But which one. That's no good. She could have flown with any of half a dozen different airlines.

Phone hospitals. That would take ages. Who else would know? He was beginning to panic. The two women looked on, clearly worried for the nice young man.

He turned to face the women again.

'I don't know what to do. Lydia is my fiancée as well as my secretary. I'm very worried about her. Have you any idea what I could do?'

'Oh dear, I am sorry,' said Monica, touching Steve's arm. 'I don't know. What do you think, Elsie?' she said, turning to her friend.

'What about the police? They would know if there'd been an accident. I hope there hasn't of course, oh dear!'

'Good idea, of course, thank you. Why didn't I think of that?'

Elsie smiled, pleased she'd been a help.

Steven phoned the police. They said they would enquire and get back to him. But he was impatient. He could not just sit and wait.

# 30

Steven reasoned that his MI5 colleagues were the ideal people to find Lydia. Could he use the emergency phone number? Better not.

It wasn't much over an hour and a half drive to Chalgrove and driving would take his mind off the problem for a while. It didn't, but he felt better to be doing something, and he did enjoy driving the Porche, even in these circumstances.

William greeted him at the unmarked office door.

'Hello, old man. Keen to get back into action so soon? Come on in, we'll see what we can find for you. What do you fancy, another assassination?'

'Just listen to me a minute, please, William. I have a problem.'

Sensing that this was not a time for jokes, William led Steven into the office. He called Bernard.

'What's the problem?' asked Bernard, seriously.

'Lydia has gone missing.'

'How come?' asked William and Bernard together.

Steven explained how Lydia had had found out where he and Mario were working and had come out to Serbia to find them, and had been sent back.

'She sounds like a very clever girl, the sort of person we could do with, wouldn't you say, Berard,' said William.

'Certainly, that took some brains. Anyway, you sent her packing, quite right of course. Couldn't have her cramping your style and getting into trouble.'

'I thought she would have flown back home, and when I went to her home she wasn't there. She wasn't at the office – hadn't been there all the week.'

'You think the Serbs have got her,' said Bernard.

'I'm afraid so, yes. Although I can't think how they could have made the connection.'

'Looks like you'll have to go back. But this time they know who you are. It will be very dangerous. If I had another agent out there, I wouldn't let you go, but I haven't. The nearest guy is 597 and he's in Vienna.'

'How long would it take 597 to get to Belgrade?' William asked.

'Flying would be quickest, if there's a convenient flight; it's only just over an hour. The bus takes a bit longer, but again that's only if there's a bus going when you want it. Same goes for trains although they are quite frequent. Best bet would be to drive, couple of hours maybe. 597 has a car out there. He could be in Belgrade by teatime.'

'Great Scott, you are a walking Bradshaw's!' exclaimed William. 'How do you know all that, old man?'

'When I was covering that business in Belgrade a few years ago, I had a girlfriend in Austria.' Bernard chuckled.

'You old devil you!' said William, also chuckling.

'Look, do you mind, this is serious. Will you get Heinz fifty-seven to investigate for me?' Steven interrupted.

'Of course. I apologise. I think he's finished what he was sent out there to do, so he'll be free. I'll get on to him straight away.'

'Can I go as well?' Steven ventured. 'I'll go mad if I'm not doing something myself.'

'Wouldn't normally allow it when there's a personal interest, but, yes. OK, with our full backing. '

'Thank you, Bernard. I appreciate it.'

'What are you like at parachuting? Did you do the course?'

'Parachuting? No, I didn't. I'm not sure I like the idea.'

'It would get you there very quickly, that's for sure.' William was smiling, but it was not a mirthful smile.

'In that case,' said Steven, hesitating sightly, 'When can you arrange it?'

'Why do you think we have an office on an airfield? I can arrange emergency drops almost immediately. What do you need to take?'

'I have a small bag with essentials in the car. I hope I shan't have to stay overnight.'

'Got your gun?'

'Of course!'

'Did you remember to replace the shells you used?'

'Of course!'

'Spare mags?'

'Yes, and I have the fourteen round mags this time. Just in case.'

'Good man!' said Bernad. OK then. Ten minutes?' He left the office, causing something of a vacuum.

Ten minutes later, Bernard reappeared holding a parachute and Steven's overnight bag, retrieved from his car.

He quickly went through the procedure of the jump and how to land safely. Steven hoped he would remember.

'Get yourself into this and see me outside.'

With William's help Steven was soon waddling out to the airfield where a Pacific Aerospace P 750 XSTOL waited, its single Pratt and Whitney turbo-prop idling lumpily.

'Off you go, your pilot is a friend of mine, Jeff Weedon, good man. ETA three hours from now. Be safe old man and best of luck.' Bernard slapped

Steven hard on his back, almost knocking him over.

Steven staggered over the aircraft. There was room for many more passengers than the aeroplane was carrying today. Steven selected a seat and made himself comfortable. A flight attendant sat close, but said nothing.

Bernard was shouting over the noise of the engine, 'Forgot to say, 597 can't make it. He's been injured. You're on your own. Sorry, old chap.'

A shout from up front announced take-off imminent.

Everything had happened so quickly he'd hardly got it into his head what lay ahead. He was to be dropped out of an aeroplane into a country he was unfamiliar with, never having even thought about parachuting until ten minutes ago. His head was spinning. He was happy flying, that wasn't a problem. The more he thought about jumping out of the plane, he more he didn't like the idea. But if he was going to find Lydia, then he would do anything.

He thought about wartime spies dropping from Lysanders into enemy territory. But was this all that different? He was a spy and he was dropping into Mafia country and they were every bit as scary as Nazis. Not as many of them, but similar consequences if you got caught.

Thinking like this is not helping, he said to himself. But he couldn't help himself.  Three hours like this. He would be a nervous wreck before he even jumped out of the aircraft.

Mercifully he slept, and only woke when the flight attendant prodded him to tell him they were approaching the drop zone.

Bernard, who knew the city well, had chosen the football stadium for Steven's drop. It would be in the early hours of the morning so should be quiet and dark. He said it was about a forty-minute walk into the city centre and advised against using a taxi, even if there was one available. It was vital that his arrival remained secret.

The large door of the aircraft had been open for several minutes. Steven stood looking out into the darkness. The cold wind did nothing to help. The flight attendant, who was dressed a civilian, held Steven's arm. Steven guessed he was one of Bernard's staff.

A strap attached to a rail by the door and connected to his parachute would open the chute as soon as he was clear of the aircraft. One less thing to worry about. But he still had lots of things to remember.

'Go, go, go!' shouted the flight attendant, giving Steven a hefty push.

The initial sensation of falling and the intense rush of cold air took his breath. He was too terrified to think.

Then suddenly, it felt as if he was going up rather than down as the parachute opened with a crack. The straps bit painfully into his crotch. But then all was calm. He could see the oval shape of the stadium below. The pilot had navigated accurately. He was descending at a comfortable rate. He tried to remember the drill that he'd been taught minutes before take-off. Supposing he broke a leg, then what would happen? Best not think about it.

Bang! He was on the ground, frantically checking himself for injuries and gathering up the folds of fabric.

The stadium was in darkness, but he could see pinpricks of light in places; exits possibly.

Once he had stuffed the parachute into the bag provided, he looked for somewhere to hide it.

Large litter bins were placed at intervals around the stadium. Just big enough into which to stuff the chute.

He cautiously explored possible exit points. The gates would surely be locked; it was not going to be easy.

There were turnstiles at all the entrances, and they would not move. He was beginning to panic. To go through the trauma of jumping out of an aeroplane and then be thwarted by locked gates was too much.

The sound of an engine close by suggested there was a vehicular entrance. A large truck entered the stadium at the far end and several men jumped out. Maintenance men no doubt, thought Steven.

He had to get to the exit before it closed again without being seen by the men who were now moving in different directions in the stadium.

He crept along the perimeter wall of the playing area, hoping he could not be seen. Then suddenly all the floodlights came on, throwing everything into stark contrast. Steven felt like a target, but there was no shout. Nobody seemed to have seen him. He carried on towards the truck, which had already turned round and was heading for the exit.

He ran the last twenty yards and just made it before the big gates closed. Gasping for breath, he stood in shadow just outside the gate for several minutes. There was nobody about. The truck had driven off, unaware of his presence. He could hardly believe his luck.

# 31

The walk into the city centre took more than Bernard's estimated forty minutes, but it was less than an hour later when he approached the reception desk of the Golden Tulip Hotel once more. It was still only four-thirty in the morning.

'Oh, hello, Mr Stansgate, back so soon?'

'Yes, something came up. Could I possibly have the same room again for a few days? I can't say exactly.

'No problem at all, sir. Do you have any luggage?'

'It will be here later. Nothing just now, apart from this,' he patted the small overnight bag that held all his needs for a few days.

'I'll get the porter to show you to your room.'

'No need, I know where it is.'

'Of course. Would you mind signing the register.'

The receptionist had put him at ease so much he almost signed his real name.

'Oh, I almost forgot – has Miss Fowler booked in?'

'Miss Fowler, sir?'

'Yes, my fiancée, she was with me last week, remember?'

'Ah, yes, I remember the young lady. No, she checked out before you, I believe.'

'Yes, she did, but I'm expecting her back.'

'I have not seen her since then. I will check with the other receptionists.'

'Would you? That's very kind.'

'Not at all, sir. Is there anything else I can help you with?'

'Is room service available this early?'

'Any time, sir, day or night. What would you like. I will get it for you.'

'Some sandwiches and bottle of red wine then. Thank you.'

'Very good, sir.'

Sitting in his hotel room eating ham sandwiches and drinking a very nice Knyazeva red, it could all have felt very civilised. But Steven had too much on his mind to be able to enjoy the food. He was worried sick about Lydia. He had no idea where to start looking for her.

News travels fast in the Mafia. How they knew he was there was a mystery, but they did. The message pushed under his hotel room door confirmed it.

*We have your woman. Get out of Belgrade. Take nose out of business. Do not contact police. She will return to you. Failure to comply will result in death. You and girl.*

Steven read and reread the message several times.

What could he do? He had no friends in Serbia, no one to whom he could turn to and talk through his problem. He had only just arrived, and to be confronted with an ultimatum like this was devastating.

He had hardly had time to digest the threat when a knock at the door made him grab his gun – his only ally.

'Yes? Who is it?' he said to the closed door.

'Open door!' came the voice in heavily accented menace.

Keeping his gun aimed at the entrance, he opened the door. Two men barged into the room, both had large automatic weapons aimed at Steven.

'You will not need gun. We have two!' said the larger of the two men, smiling. 'Please put down, and sit. We not kill you.'

Steven sat, and put his gun on a side table. The smaller of the two men picked it up and put it in his pocket. He smiled too. It was disconcerting.

'Now, Mr Sebworth,' said the larger man, smiling again, 'yes, we know who you are. We have your girlfriend. She is safe and well. We have not harmed her. She is nice, yes?' he smiled again.

'My name, Otto, him is Grock. We don't like people interfering with our business, you understand. Nothing personal, but we need you to leave Serbia. We have good system here. People do as told, all good. If not do as told, they regret. You understand of course, Mr Sebworth.'

Steven didn't answer.

Otto hit the table next to Steven with his gun, making Steven jump. 'Understand?' he said, sharply.

'Yes, yes, I understand,' said Steven, feebly.

'Good, we have understanding, is good, yes?'

'Yes,' said Steven, nodding.

'So, you go. We take to airport. Your girl follow.'

'How do I know you will let her go?'

'Oh, Mr Sebworth, you not trust us?' he was smiling again. Steven wished he wouldn't.

There was absolutely nothing he could do in these circumstances. He had no doubt they meant it when they said they would kill him and Lydia if he didn't do as he was told. He daren't risk Lydia's life.

'OK, let's go,' said the spokesman.

Grock led the way, Steven and Otto left the room, arm in arm. Looking friendly.

'You off again, so soon, Mr Stansgate!' called the receptionist when he saw the trio heading for the way out.

'Fraid so! Bye!' Steven called. Thinking perhaps the man would suspect something amiss. But then, it would not help if he called the police.

A big Aurus Senat limousine, the same type of car used by Russian leaders, whisked them silently to the airport, where Otto went to book a flight to

Heathrow. He came back to Steven and Grock, smiling, and handed Steven his ticket.

Suddenly, a quartet of uniformed men brandishing Heckler und Koch submachine guns, appeared from nowhere and surrounded Steven and his captors. Otto and Grock were soon disarmed and led away. Steven tried to explain what might happen, but his rescuers did not understand.

While Steven was trying to speak to one of the men, Mario appeared grinning. 'Saved by the bell, eh, old man?'

'Oh, Good Grief, Mario. Where did you spring from? Listen, you've put Lydia in terrible danger by intervening.' He quickly explained the situation to Mario, who translated for the Serbian officer, who spoke German. Between them they understood what had happened, but didn't have any answers.

'We have to convince the bad guys that I've left the country and that this was all a mistake. Let Otto and Grock go. They will report back that I've gone and with luck they'll let Lydia go.'

'Otto and Grock? You're joking. No, you're not, sorry. OK, I get it. Leave it with me. It will be OK.'

After a lot of muti-lingual explanation Mario was able to convince the police to release Otto and Grock without charge.

Steven got aboard the aircraft bound for Heathrow, but managed to get off again without anyone seeing him, thanks to the assistance of the crew. He met up with Mario in the borrowed uniform of an airport worker in the restaurant. Mario handed Steven his gun, which had been taken from Otto.

'How did you manage that?' Steven asked incredulously.

Mario tapped the side of his nose.

'Now we wait,' said Steven. 'I just hope there is some decency in the heart of the Mafia, and they let her go.'

# 32

'If they let her go, what will she do? Did they say how or when or where they would release her?' asked Mario after a long silence.

'No, they didn't tell me anything. I've no idea.'

'So, think about it. Where was she when they nabbed her?'

'Here, I'd assumed.'

'But isn't it more likely they would take her to the hotel?'

'By Jove, yes, you're probably right. That's where they would have found out about her. We'd better get over there, pronto.'

'Oh, you speaka d'Italiano?' Mario jested. Steven just gave him a look that withered any more jokes on the stem.

The hotel receptionist did a double take when Steven entered the foyer, especially as he was dressed in Serbian Airport unform.

'Hello again, Mr Stansgate. How are you?'

'I'm OK, thanks. My key please.'

'Of course. By the way. The young lady is waiting for you in your room.'

'What? Miss Fowler? Oh, Man, thank you!'

'Yes, Miss Fowler, indeed, sir!' He smiled. Steven grinned, and Mario smiled, too.

We will not intrude upon their reunion; just be sure it was a happy one.